MONKEY IN THE MIDDLE

MONKEY IN THE MIDDLE

Stephen Solomita

severn
House

This first world edition published 2008
in Great Britain and the USA by
SEVERN HOUSE PUBLISHERS LTD of
9–15 High Street, Sutton, Surrey, England, SM1 1DF.

British Library Cataloguing in Publication Data

Solomita, Stephen
  Monkey in the middle
  1. Organized crime - New York (State) - New York - Fiction
  2. Police - New York (State) - New York - Fiction
  3. Detective and mystery stories
  I. Title
  813.5'4[F]

  ISBN-13: 978-0-7278-6634-9   (cased)
  ISBN-13: 978-1-84751-065-5   (trade paper)

All Severn House titles are printed on acid-free paper.

Typeset by Palimpsest Book Production Ltd.,
Grangemouth, Stirlingshire, Scotland.
Printed and bound in Great Britain by
MPG Books Ltd., Bodmin, Cornwall.

for Miriam Joseph,
constant companion

One

L eonard Carter is overwhelmed at first, a matter of too
  much input. Evergreen branches wound with Christmas-
red ribbon form a series of receding arches that run the
length of the floor. Red, white, pink and yellow poinsettias
crowd the top of every kiosk. A Christmas tree of red poinsettias rises twenty feet to the ceiling; its flaming leaves
match the color of the ribbon exactly. Merchandise glitters
on either side of the long aisle, display cases piled with
jewelry, leather handbags on racks, perfume and cosmetics.
Along a center beam, massive light fixtures telescope from
the ceiling. They beckon to Carter like points on a treasure
map, like the song pouring from hidden speakers at deafening volume. Burl Ives doing *Holly Jolly Christmas*.

A full minute passes before Carter becomes aware of the
swarm buzzing around him, of the goggle-eyed shoppers
who brush against his shoulders as they pass. He tries to
laugh, but fails. Then he cops to the reality: he was so
focused on the mark that he walked through the Sixth
Avenue entrance to Macy's, five days before Christmas, as
though anticipating an empty room. This is not something
he can toss off with a laugh.

The steady drone of conversation and the relentless music,
along with the blended odors of perfume and powder and
bodies sweating beneath heavy coats, flood Carter's awareness, as physical as onrushing surf. For a moment, Carter
thinks that he's the object of the crowd's nervous chatter,
a Frankenstein to their peasant mob.

'You gonna just fuckin' stand there?'

Carter turns to find a Latino woman pushing a stroller.
For the length of a thought, he sees, as vividly as in a dream,

the blade of a knife slicing across her throat. Then he steps to the side, turning his face away.

'Sorry.'

The encounter sobers Leonard Carter. He asks himself, What did you expect? But then he puts a name to it: slippage. That's what he calls his lapse. Slippage. And not for the first time.

Carter is wearing a gray fedora with a little feather in its band. Without raising his head, he peers from beneath the hat's four-inch brim. The store's decorations intrigue him, especially the receding arches, which are not wrapped with ribbon as he'd originally thought, but covered with bows so cleverly placed they seem to form a perfect spiral. And now that he's really looking, he finds Christmas ornaments and tiny Christmas lights, and he notices that the curve of each arch is virtually identical to all the others.

Precision has always appealed to Carter, from his earliest days. He believes there's a right way to do things. Finding it? Maybe that's a horse of a different color. Maybe you can search for your entire life and never find the right way. That doesn't mean it isn't out there.

Sometimes, Carter believes that efficiency is a form of worship. This is never more true than when he handles weapons. Carter's ability to field-strip his rifle, to lay out the parts exactly as the sergeant instructed, won him nominations, to the Army Rangers, and then to the super-secret Delta Force. Carter had gone along with the program, but not because he was ambitious. The simple truth was that the army had it right and there was no reason to improvise. The way Carter arranged the various components when he disassembled his weapon, each element fell to hand exactly as needed when the time came to put it back together. His fingers seemed to move by themselves, he no more than a neutral observer.

Suddenly, Carter realizes that he's lost sight of the mark. More slippage. But this time he smiles to himself. There's no rush. If not today, tomorrow.

Swept along by the crowds, Carter meanders into a side aisle. Here, the evergreen boughs are penetrated by thousands of Christmas lights. The lights don't follow a rigid pattern, yet their careful placement is obvious. There are no bare spots and no clusters. Same for the ornaments. All bear testimony to a careful hand.

A few yards ahead, a woman sits on a stool before a cosmetics counter, a white towel covering her shoulders. The woman is just a step short of elderly and her bony face is well lined. Carter wonders what she hopes to accomplish. Simple dignity, that would be her best bet. Meanwhile, the splotches of rouge applied to her cheeks by a beautician young enough to be her grandchild, applied over a layer of powder as thick and stiff as porcelain, are just a shade less garish than the poinsettia leaves.

'I don't know . . . What do you think? Is it too much?'

The beautician gives her platinum blonde hair a professional shake. She cocks her head, closes one blue eye, then nods wisely.

'You go for it, girl.'

As much as possible, Carter avoids physical contact with strangers, a matter of instinct. But that's not possible here. The shoppers, adults and children alike, wander as if in a trance, lurching right and left, stopping dead in their tracks, heads swiveling like radar discs sweeping a horizon. Carter has to force his way into the center aisle, another affront. Civility is what makes the world go round, especially in cities as insanely crowded as New York. What he now observes is a form of anarchy.

'Excuse me,' Carter says to an obese man wearing a bomber jacket that proclaims 'BLUE DEVILS RULE'. The man doesn't respond and Carter's first instinct is to drive his fist into the man's kidney. He is about to do so when he spots the mark thirty feet away.

Ashamed, Carter jams his clenched fist into his pocket. For a moment, he'd forgotten all about the mark, or even why he was in Macy's in the first place. More slippage.

Heh-heh.

Carter moves closer to a display case. Diamonds illuminated by pinpoint lights flash a cold fire. He draws a breath through his nose, feels it slither down the back of his throat and into his lungs, warm and fragrant. He's home now.

The mark is examining women's watches, one after another. The open boxes on the counter reveal labels: Bulova, Movado, ESQ Swiss, Seiko. Carter resists an urge to straighten the boxes, to arrange them in a line with the center box slightly forward. He drops to one knee and feigns interest in a two carat engagement ring.

Carter knows the mark, whose name is Anthony Maguire, fairly well. He has a wife, three children, a legit business (Empire Construction), and a bookmaking operation run from a bar on Northern Boulevard in Roslyn. High school educated, Maguire is the proud owner of season tickets to all New York Giants' home games, a man who eats hamburgers seated at the bar, a man who likes to talk. Even now, his lips move rapidly as he chats up the clerk, a black girl less than half his age. Six and a half feet tall, he makes for an imposing figure, leaning across the counter, near enough for the girl to feel his breath against her forehead. And that's another thing about Anthony Maguire. Though he supports a wife, three children, his aging mother and a full-time mistress named Zenia, he comes on to every woman who crosses his path.

Carter straightens. He wills himself to become part of the scene, an automaton among automatons, pre-programmed to observe an elaborate, ongoing ritual. A lifetime before, in Africa during the worst-of-the-worst, Ranan Barad described the Nataraja dance of the Hindu god Shiva. All of creation and all of destruction, Ranan explained, is contained in this dance: the crackling fire, the Milky Way, bright enough in the African sky to be itself a god. Even the men who would hack them to death are in this dance. Even the amphetamines that keep them awake and alive.

The mark shakes his head, then turns and takes a step toward Carter. His coat and jacket are open, his gut protruding. Carter pulls the dagger from its sheath at his belt. He balances the hilt on the tips of his fingers, leaving the blade to rest against his forearm. The mark's gait is noticeably splay-footed and he walks with his shoulders back, his arms hanging loosely at his sides. All to the good.

Carter focuses on a single polka dot on the mark's tie. As he moves to the man's right, then comes forward, he imagines the precise arc which will carry the dagger to this point, the rotation of his shoulder, his wrist flipping out to expose the blade (but only for an instant), his elbow held as close to his ribs as possible.

His body repeats the imagined sequence at the very last moment. Just as he and the mark are about to pass, the dagger's blade strikes a point an inch below the mark's sternum, driving through a thick layer of fat, through the muscles of the diaphragm, into the major blood vessels beneath.

There is no blood, and there won't be until the knife is pulled out.

The mark grunts when the knife pierces his flesh, but makes no other sound. His diaphragm is temporarily paralyzed and he can neither draw nor expel breath. An instant before he crashes to the floor, he seizes the dagger's grip with both hands, effectively concealing its existence.

The shoppers closest to him instinctively recoil, as though he carries some terrible and contagious disease. But they don't scatter. Instead, suddenly curious, they form a circle around him, nobody making a move until a security guard rushes up.

'Are you all right, sir?' the man asks just as the mark yanks the dagger out. 'Are you all right?'

A river of blood answers his question.

Two

Carter skips the dramatics. His business completed, he walks, supremely casual, down the aisle, through Macy's Seventh Avenue addition, finally out on to the street. More crowds, more sleep-walking tourists wobbling along the sidewalk like drunks in a silent movie. A Salvation Army Santa – a black man with the bony face of an Abe Lincoln – tolls a bell and mutters Merry Christmas over and over again. His eyes are fixed on some distant shore and his voice is without inflection. His bell rises and falls, regular as a metronome: *da-ding . . . da-ding . . . da-ding . . . da-ding.* Carter's dollar, tossed into his red kettle, elicits no response.

Carter rides the 1 Train up to Columbus Circle, then walks the few blocks to the Orchid Hotel where he finds a men's room on the lobby floor. Inside a stall, he removes the wig and the false beard he wears, tossing them, along with his fedora, into a white garbage bag taken from his coat pocket. A few minutes later, he dumps the bag into a trash can on Sixty-Fourth Street, a can standing at the curb, ready for pick-up. Finally, Carter hails a cab.

The late afternoon traffic is predictably heavy and Carter spends the next forty-five minutes staring through dirty glass at dirty cars, trucks and busses, dirty streets, dirty sidewalks. The driver curses occasionally, but spends most of his time on a cell phone, rattling away in Arabic. Carter has heard Arabic before; he can even speak a few words: raise your hands, shut-up, get on the ground, I'm gonna cut off your balls and eat them. These are phrases he picked up questioning foreign fighters in Afghanistan, then used to good effect while employed by Coldstream Military Options in Iraq.

Carter has never liked Arabic, the harsh consonants, the machine-gun speed, every word an assault. Even when they're happy, Arabs spit out their words. But he didn't much like Arabs in general. One minute they were your friend, the next your enemy. When he became a mercenary, he was told, by the man who hired him, to beware of the Iraqis in his company.

'They'll call you their brother, share their food, drink from your bottle, then set you up a few months down the road. In their little world, if you're not family, clan or tribe, you're nothing.'

For Carter, who didn't trust the man offering the good advice, suspicion was not a problem.

The driver pulls to the curb at Avenue B and Fifth Street on the Lower East Side of Manhattan. Carter pays him off, then hustles into the Cabrini Center for Nursing and Rehabilitation. A security guard named Sam waves a hello. Sam is seated behind a desk, his eyes tracking a series of monitors while he mans a cell phone.

'C'mon, Gloria, this bullshit has got to stop. So, the boy tore his pants. That's just how boys do.'

Carter returns Sam's wave, then sprints up two flights of stairs to room 306. The room contains a pair of beds. One of them is empty, its occupant currently in the hospital but expected to return. The other holds a woman named Jane Carter. Jane is Carter's sister.

'You awake, Janie?'

Jane's eyelids part and she blinks once. She's a large woman, tall and broad enough to almost fill the narrow bed. Nevertheless, except for the rise and fall of her ribcage when a ventilator forces breath upon her, she lies unmoving beneath the blankets. Jane's face is slack as well, the muscles flaccid, but her cheeks are pink with color and rounded.

'I been rushin' around all day.' Carter sighs. 'Business as usual.'

Jane blinks once, in slow motion, eyelashes fluttering.

'I had a client like you wouldn't believe. The client from hell.'

Carter goes on to create a day that never happened. He's become very good at this, inventing a life for his sister's benefit, an alternative to the life he lives. In this imaginary life, he sells high-end sporting goods for a French manu-facturer, bouncing from client to client, and even from city to city.

'I swear to you, Janie, I think the guy was on speed. He couldn't stop scratching himself and his left cheek would twitch every few seconds, like twice, twitch-twitch. Now, you should understand, I was pitching the guy a new line of sports bras, so in no way did I want to get on his bad side. But the twitch was coming so regular, I found my eyes jumping up to his cheek whenever it went off. Meanwhile, the poor bastard's scratching away, his knees, his chest, the side of his neck. He's wriggling in his chair like his pants are on fire.'

Sometimes, Carter believes that he'll just fly off when Janie dies. Like in the old spiritual. But not to God. Carter thinks he'll rise up through the atmosphere and out into space like somebody cut the guy lines anchoring a weather balloon.

'You want me to read for a while?' Carter is standing by the side of the bed, speaking over the whoosh of the venti-lator. Janie's eyes track his small movements, the tilt of his chin, the nod, the shrug.

Blink.

Carter pulls a chair to the edge of the bed. He takes a bible from the nightstand and opens it to a book-marked page: Proverbs, Chapter 1. The choice of material is Janie's.

Carter has read a number of books to his sister over the past two years and this is his second time through the bible. He's relieved to be finished with Psalms. Let's make a deal, that's what the poems were about. I'll do this for you, God, if you do that for me. The howl of outrage when God didn't come across was deafening. I said all the prayers, performed all the rituals. I kissed your ass from morning till night. Now my enemies are beating me into the ground and it's your fault?

'The parables of Solomon, the son of David, king of

Israel. To know wisdom, and instruction; to understand the words of prudence, and to receive the instruction of doctrine, justice and judgment, and equity; to give subtlety to little ones, to the young man knowledge and understanding. A wise man shall hear and be wiser; and he that understandeth shall possess governments . . .'

The stench of human waste rises suddenly to Carter's nostrils. This is the second time in the last three days and he's not ready to go home. He closes the bible and stands. Janie is lying exactly as she was, only her eyes have turned away. She will not look at him now.

'You want me to call the aide?'

Blink.

'You want me to leave?'

Blink.

Three

Carter boards the N Train at Eighth Street and settles in for the ride out to Newtown Avenue in the Queens neighborhood of Astoria. He finds a seat on a long bench, crosses his legs, folds his hands in his lap. Though Carter takes great care to present the world with an instantly forgettable persona, the man who is not there, his conscious aim is to be acutely aware of his surroundings. But this time his attention drifts as the train rumbles through Manhattan, describing a long arc that takes it as far west as Seventh Avenue.

Janie's shame has unsettled Carter. Her shame has become his guilt. Carter had been drifting through Africa when Janie's illness was first diagnosed. He continued to drift for two years afterward, first through Sierra Leone, the Ivory Coast and Liberia, then south to Angola and the Congo. Working for anybody who'd have him, doing whatever he was told. He might have come back at any time. No shackles bound him to the carnage. Instead he chased . . . Chased what?

But that's just it. Carter can no longer answer this question. Diamonds, that's how he would have responded if asked even six months before, the pot of gold at the end of the bloodiest rainbow on the planet. And blood there was. An ocean of blood, the locals reduced to slavery, the women with no hands, no arms, no feet, twelve-year-old soldiers high on kaat wielding fully-automatic Kalishnikovs. Children mutilating children.

It was all a video game to the boy soldiers, right up until they squared off against battle-hardened professionals like Carter. Then they threw down their weapons and their young bodies trembled and their eyes turned inward. And when they finally realized there were no rules and the bloody-thirsty god they served would drink their blood as well, they cried like babies.

A rapping on the floor at the other end of the car jolts Carter's awareness. A man in his mid-twenties with a cane and no sign of a limp, glancing around before again jabbing the cane into the floor.

Bap, bap, bap.

Without looking directly at the man, Carter takes inventory. He registers a white male, five-ten, maybe 190 pounds, his greasy blond dreadlocks partially concealed by a baseball hat with a torn brim. Despite the cold, the man wears short pants that cover his knees, a hooded sweatshirt and low-top basketball shoes without socks. His face is big and square, his cheeks pitted. His fixed smirk, the mark of a bully, is instantly recognized by Carter.

Bap, bap, bap.

The passengers closest to the man huddle in their seats, eyes fixed to the ceiling or floor. His behavior diminishes them. He takes their space and awards it to himself. And if they don't like it . . .

Carter doesn't know when the man got on the train. An oversight, ha-ha. More slippage. There was a time when his own shadow couldn't sneak up on him.

Bap, bap, bap.

Dropping his elbows to his knees, Carter leans forward, drawing the attention of the man at the other end of the car. The man looks at Carter, then turns away, his smirk vanishing as if he's read Carter's mind in that brief moment.

How easy, Carter is thinking, how easy it would be to kill this man, how easy, easy, easy, easy, easy . . .

After locking the door to his apartment, Carter turns on his computer. When prompted, he enters a password that allows him access to the hard drive: @e4oIBn3o87y5()&. Memorizing this password took nearly a week, but the result is worth the effort. This level of encryption will frustrate any government agency short of NASA. Or so Thorpe claimed when he insisted that Carter install the program.

Thorpe is even more paranoid than Carter, which is the only thing Carter likes about him. Except for the money, of course, and the jobs that lead to the money.

Speaking of which . . .

Carter's e-mail is one sentence long: *The deed is done.* With a single click, he sends it off to a computer in Rumania. From there, it will find its way to Thorpe, who might be anywhere in the world, who might be living next door. Thorpe will respond by dropping $20,000 into Carter's bank account on the island of Jamaica. And promptly, too.

But not this time. As Carter goes to shut his computer down, the machine emits a sharp ding. Then a little envelope appears at the top right of the monitor. The envelope waves at him.

Thorpe's message is not as simple as Carter's: *The deed is NOT done, though perhaps well on its way to being done. Suggest you proceed to next stage. Also, FYI, contract terms are strict. Payment on closing only. Please advise as events transpire.*

Slippage? Carter closes his eyes for a moment, remembering the knife's arc, the blade punching through the soft flesh just below the sternum, the descending aorta only a few inches away. Cutting a vessel of this size results in more rapid blood loss than a similar injury to the heart, and there are no ribs to avoid.

So, he must have missed. To the right, the left, low, high? Carter goes online, to the homepage of the *Daily News* where he scans the longest of several stories on the 'Macy's Mayhem'. The victim, he learns, is still alive, though in a critical condition, and the cops think it likely that he was targeted by a deranged man, perhaps one of the many homeless schizophrenics who roam the city. Nevertheless, the victim's room at Bellevue Hospital is being closely guarded, just in case.

Carter shuts down the computer, then swivels his chair in a half-circle to face a largely empty room. There's the computer station, a neatly-made bed, a nightstand bearing a small lamp, and that's it. The spotless walls are blank rectangles, while the gleaming parquet floors are without rugs.

Carter's clothes are stored in labeled boxes in a closet, each item precisely folded.

Carter shrugs out of his shoes and walks over to the apartment's single bedroom. There is no bed here and the floor is covered by judo mats. At the doorway, he takes a moment to center himself, then strips to his shorts before approaching a table with a long wooden box on top. Here he again pauses, staring down.

The box's elaborate carvings include every large animal on the African savannah. The reproductions are crude by western standards, but Carter believes they are designed to illustrate the spirits that inhabit the creatures, not the creatures themselves. The box's maker was endowing his creation with power. The other part, a symmetry so exquisitely planned the overall design had seemed abstract the first time Carter saw it, was a secondary consideration. As was the wood chosen to construct the box, black ebony hard enough to ward off decay and termites both.

When Carter flicks a switch on the wall, two rows of tightly focused spotlights, mounted on tracks, throw small circles of light on the floor. Carter adjusts three of these lights, then opens the box to reveal a pair of Burmese daggers. Carved into fire-breathing dragons from blocks of white jade, the daggers are intended for ceremonial use and that is the way Carter has always used them. The dragons' arched heads and necks form the daggers' pommels, their bodies the handles, their wings the guards, their tails the blades. Though exquisitely crafted, the daggers are not antiques. Even so, in order to possess them, Carter had to surrender a big chunk of the pile he accumulated in Africa.

Carter takes the daggers and crosses them over his chest with the points to the sides of his throat. He turns slowly, his eyes moving to each of the little circles of light. These are the marks he will hit as he crisscrosses the room.

There are no stops in Carter's workout, no poses, no pauses. Taught to him in Freetown by a fellow mercenary, the techniques he will use are adapted from Sinawali, a martial arts system developed in the Philippines. Sinawali means woven, and this is what Carter accomplishes, effortlessly weaving defense and attack into a continuous movement, his footwork taking him across the floor. Carter is not a large man. His shoulders are not especially wide or his back especially broad. But he is heavily muscled and extremely graceful. In his hands, the jade daggers appear to liquefy, to leave a luminescent trail not unlike the glistening track left on wet grass by a passing snail.

Four

S olly Epstein hesitates outside the crime scene tape. He
shoves his hands into the pockets of his camel hair coat
and hunches his shoulders against the wind. Epstein's shoulders are massive, seemingly misplaced on the body of a
man five feet, eight inches tall. His back is outsized as well,
his neck too. Except for the rounded gut, bandy legs and
the rapidly balding dome, he might be a diminutive version
of the Amazing Hulk.

Before him, the façade of Macy's flagship store spans
the short block along Broadway between Thirty-Third and
Thirty-Fourth Streets. Epstein is something of a New York
buff and he considers Macy's, with its Thanksgiving Day
Parade, Fourth of July fireworks and Christmas decorations,
as much a part of the city's life as the Empire State Building
or the Stock Exchange. The store's windows are especially
renowned and no tourist in New York at Christmas passes
up an opportunity to view them.

This year's windows are no exception: flying dragons, a
roaring lion (Aslan of Narnia? Epstein isn't sure), Harry
Potter sweeping across the rooftops of London. The detail
is astounding. Every millimeter of the back wall is covered,
the floor and the ceiling as well. The colors are bright,
primary, and the effect is magical, a demand that he revisit
his childhood, that he become once more innocent. This
effect is made all the more powerful by an anomaly. On
any other day the crowds would be six deep with the luck-
iest kids astride their daddies' shoulders. Now the sidewalk
is part of a crime scene, the space before the windows
empty, as if they were meant only for him.

Suddenly embarrassed, Epstein glances up. A dozen

helicopters hover overhead. The reporters have to be loving this, he thinks. And they'll be loving it even more when the name of the victim is released and they find out he's a local gangster. Given this nudge, he knows, it's even possible that some enterprising scribbler will connect the death of Tony Maguire to three prior murders. The victims of these homicides, like Tony, were known members of Paul Marginella's crew. Paulie Margarine, who claims to be clueless but who's about to start a war.

Epstein clips his badge to the lapel of his jacket, then approaches a cop doing sentry duty at a break in the crime scene tape blocking off the sidewalk. He flips open a billfold to reveal his ID: Lieutenant Solomon Epstein, Organized Crime Control Bureau. The uniform logs the information, along with the time of day.

'Anybody else here from OCCB?' Epstein asks.

The cop's finger trails backward through his chart. 'Sergeant Boyle. Arrived thirty minutes ago.'

'Good.'

With the obsessively competent Billy Boyle on the scene, Epstein won't have to sweat the details. Epstein isn't averse to details, but he prefers to have others collect, sort and label them before he considers their implications.

The store's interior decorations stop Epstein, as they did Carter. Elsewhere, in more upscale department stores, the overall scheme is resolutely cool. White lights and pale ribbon, greens and pinks, nobody getting too excited. After all, it's only Christmas. Not so Macy's. Much to Epstein's satisfaction, Macy's showroom is pure Christmas overkill, the red of the poinsettias as garish as onrushing blood.

In Epstein's opinion, Christmas is all about overkill. When his son is finally born, Epstein will cover the boy's first Christmas tree with red and green and blue and yellow lights. He'll fill the branches with ornaments, crown the tree with a golden angel, stack presents to the ceiling.

Though Epstein's father was Jewish, he was raised by his Italian-Irish mother, his old man having fled the scene before Epstein's first birthday.

Epstein fiddles in his pocket, finds his cell phone and speed-dials his wife, Sofia.

'Yo, gringo,' she says when she hears his voice.

'I just wanted to let you know that I'm on the scene. I'm gonna be tied up for a while.'

'Don't worry. Nothing's happening.' Sofia is two weeks past her due date and the doctors are threatening to induce labor if she doesn't give birth soon. 'If it does, I'll call you first.'

'Call me second, after you call your sister for a ride to the hospital. And don't be a martyr. I know you. Macho is in your blood.'

'Bye, honey.'

Epstein hesitates a second longer, to admire a half-dozen cops from the Crime Scene Unit in their white paper suits. They've fanned out from a pool of blood and are now dusting the many display cases with black fingerprint powder. At the end of the room, a pair of uniformed officers have the witnesses nicely corralled. Billy Boyle is standing a few feet away, notebook in hand, questioning a middle-aged woman in a navy business suit.

When Boyle finishes up with the witness, he turns to face his oncoming commander. As always, Boyle's nicely tailored black suit is immaculate, his red tie perfectly knotted; the starched collar of his white shirt all but stands up and salutes. Epstein appreciates the effort but considers it wasted. Bailey's face looks like it was reassembled in the dark by a first year surgical resident after going through a brick wall. Heavy bones at weird angles, or pushed to one side, nose going one way, chin the other. This is the guy you didn't want to meet near the East Side docks after midnight. Say in 1855.

'Lieutenant,' Boyle says.

'Billy.'

Boyle stares at Epstein through eyes the color of wet mud. 'Our boy fucked up this time.' He sweeps his arm in a long arc to indicate all three aisles of the immense room. 'Surveillance cameras. Every fuckin' inch. They got a control room downstairs, monitors, the works.'

'You wanna make a bet?'

Boyle shifts his weight. He raises his chin to stare along the length of a short, flat nose. 'Bet about what?'

'About whether our boy fucked up.'

Boyle ponders Epstein's offer, then shakes his head. 'Man, I hope you're right, because this bullshit is not gonna go away.'

Epstein shrugs. 'Anything else I should know?'

'I checked out the murder weapon. A dagger, double-edged, with an ivory handle. The handle's inscribed in Arabic.'

'Arabic? How do you know?'

'A stock clerk named Massoud, originally from Lebanon.'

'You showed him the murder weapon?'

'Yeah. According to Massoud, it says, "War is deception." A quote from the prophet.'

You have to admire the son-of-a-bitch, and Epstein truly does. Epstein is in Macy's basement, in a suite of rooms dedicated to the store's security functions. He stands next to Macy's head of security, a retired NYPD captain named Curt Majalewski. Behind them, Billy Boyle hovers, his arms folded across his chest.

Seated before a bank of eight small monitors, a technician guides them through Carter's every move. Epstein sees Carter approach and enter Macy's, meander from aisle to aisle, kneel before a jewelry counter, finally approach and stab Maguire, the movement so fast that the stop-action video barely records it. He watches Carter walk the length of the store to exit onto Seventh Avenue, just another Christmas pilgrim, a body in a crowd. Not for a moment, not even for a second, does Carter raise his head. Epstein's view is of a wide-brimmed hat and the point of a short beard, an occasional flash of cheekbone.

Coordinating the eight tapes is a tricky business and it takes almost an hour to cover the sixteen minutes Carter is inside Macy's. Epstein is impatient by the time the tech shuts down the last tape. His boss, Captain Tom Champliss, is already on-scene.

'Am I gonna be able to take the tapes with me or will I need a subpoena?' Epstein asks Majalewski.

'We're cooperating, a hundred per cent.' Majalewski has the husky voice of a long-time smoker. Broken capillaries radiate from his nose like the whiskers of cat.

'That's great. Sergeant Boyle will collect the tapes and write receipts.'

Epstein would love to rerun the tape. He hasn't got the time, but he knows that once the techs at the NYPD lab splice the footage, the squad will review the tape over and over again. As if they could reach into the monitor and yank the perpetrator out. They'll watch from the other end, too. Watch Tony Maguire progress from shopper to vegetable.

Because that's what they're saying at the hospital. Tony Maguire's brain is severely damaged and he's unlikely to recover any significant function. For all intents and purposes, Tough Tony's off the count.

This will not make Captain Champliss (known to one and all as Captain Champissy) smile. Nor will the failure of Macy's security system to record the perp's features. Epstein needs an angle to soften the blows, a line of investigation impressive enough to buy a little time, yet unlikely to produce results.

Epstein finally turns to Billy Boyle. 'I want you to collect surveillance tapes from the subway stations, uptown and downtown. Go south as far as Fourteenth Street, north to Columbus Circle.'

'You wanna get started right away?'

'Yeah, Billy, that's the whole point. But you can pull the detail if we don't have anything by tomorrow morning.'

Five

Epstein waits respectfully, hands at his sides, while Champliss consoles the store manager, Bob Kasman. Captain Champliss is all sympathy, from his watery black eyes to the palms of his extended hands. At appropriate moments, he nods, cocks his head, draws long theatrical breaths.

Rumor has it that Champliss is gay, but Epstein's not buying. Champliss is married with four children. But then again, Champliss does habitually stand with a cocked hip and his movements have a languid, feminine aspect. It's undeniable. And his pursed mouth seems perpetually disapproving. He might be a fashion designer offended by the sudden appearance of a grimy, skid row drunk. Oh God, what next?

Bob Kasman wears a beautifully tailored suit, an overly starched white-on-white shirt and a lavender tie. The cuffs of his trousers fall exactly to the tops of his shoes. To Epstein, in his tweed jacket and rumpled Dockers, Kasman seems fabricated, as if somebody started with the idea of a big-time businessman, then designed a human to fit the image. Every strand of the man's graying hair is in place.

'Can I be honest with you, Captain?' Kasman rushes ahead before Champliss can unwrap his pursed lips. 'It rained through the weekend, Friday, Saturday, Sunday. Every afternoon, a cold rain. As a direct result, our take is now fifteen per cent below last year's.' He pauses long enough to swallow. 'Bottom line, Macy's intends to cooperate fully but we need to be up and running tomorrow. If it's at all possible.'

Champliss finally gets in a word. He glances at his watch, then says, 'Have a clean-up crew at the ready. We'll be out of here by eight o'clock.'

Kasman favors Champliss with a nod, a tight-lipped smile and a manly handshake. When he marches off, Epstein approaches, his bandy-legged strut in sharp contrast with his superior's listless posturing.

'I got here as soon as I could,' he says.

'Bad news. I see it on your face.' Champliss is standing beside a floor-to-ceiling tree composed entirely of red poinsettias. He examines Epstein for a moment, a prophet in search of a sign, then sniffs, displaying another mannerism his underlings can't stand.

'I watched the video. It's useless.'

'And why is that?'

'The perp wore a wide-brimmed hat and didn't raise his head. Oh, and get this, the knife he used, it's one of a kind. Ivory handle with an inscription in Arabic. "War is deception".'

Champliss considers this information for a moment, then says, 'A message from Toufiq?'

A Moroccan Arab born in the United States, Rachid Toufiq is in line to benefit most from the ongoing damage to Paulie Margarine's crew. Or so the common wisdom has it. A striver to his bones, Toufiq has assembled a rag-tag gang from the large Arab community living in the Queens neighborhood of Astoria. Their turf is southern Astoria, near the Grand Central Parkway. To the north, Astoria is predominantly Greek and Italian, with a fair population of young professionals unable to afford Manhattan rents. This is Paulie Margarine's stomping ground.

Epstein takes one of the poinsettia leaves between his thumb and forefinger. He holds it for a second, imagining his small dining room made smaller at Christmastime by a dozen similar plants. Imagining the room virtually ablaze.

'I don't think it was an ego thing, leaving the knife,' he finally declares. 'I think he used a knife that he knew couldn't be traced. Rather than buy a knife and risk our tracking it to a particular store. Plus, you have to consider that Paulie Marginella's ready to explode. Guaranteed, if we release a description of the knife, he'll start a war.'

But Champliss isn't having it. 'A few days from now, if

you don't have a suspect in custody, we're going to put that knife before the public. I want it to lead the news on every channel. I want it on the front page of every newspaper. No man could own a knife like the one you described and not show it to somebody.'

Epstein doesn't argue the point, though he'd readily bet his next paycheck against a psychopath's word of honor that the knife won't be traced to the man who stuck it in Tony Maguire. Not through publicity. But a clue is a clue, and this particular clue is as photogenic as clues get. The media will eat it up.

'One more thing, Captain.' Epstein gestures to a display case fifteen feet away. 'The perp knelt in front of that case. He may have touched it, the video isn't clear, or he may have breathed on it and left DNA. I already conferred with Sergeant Washington. He's gonna take it into the lab.'

Sgt. Vernon Washington is supervising the Crime Scene Unit. The collection of trace evidence is his responsibility. OCCB has no juice here.

'The whole thing?'

'No, just the part in front of the diamonds.'

'That's impossible.'

'Impossible? Washington's already called for a truck.' Epstein looks down at his watch. 'The way it's shaping up, CSU's gonna be working all night.'

Champliss takes the news without flinching. Much to his credit, Epstein decides. Despite his peers' general disdain, Champliss is a problem-solver. Most likely, he's already composed an explanation for Kasman.

'What about witnesses?' Champliss asks.

'As it turns out, there aren't any.'

'How's that?'

'We questioned every clerk on the floor at the time of the attack. What came back is simple and consistent. The sales floor was packed and nobody noticed the vic until he grabbed his chest and fell to the floor. Heart attack – that was their first thought, and one of them actually went for a defibrillator. Then the vic yanked the knife out and they saw the blood and after that it was all panic. As for the actual attack, it's strictly *nada*. As in nobody saw nothin'.'

'What about the customers?' Champliss sweeps the room with his hand, describing a delicate arc that draws Epstein's attention. 'There had to be a couple of hundred people in here.'

'Gone before the first responders arrived. We can make a plea for witnesses to come forward when we do the press conference, but I wouldn't hold my breath.' Epstein averts his eyes, a gesture he believes appropriate in light of their respective ranks. If their positions were reversed, he thinks, he might well invoke the cliché, the one about killing the messenger. But Champliss surprises him. When Epstein looks up, his boss's prissy mouth has tightened and his black eyes might be carved from ebony.

'Grab one of Rachid Toufiq's people. Reach as high up the food chain as possible. I want you to sweat him, Solly. I want you to send a message. This has got to stop.'

Six

They grab Ibrahim El-Shaer in front of a coffee shop on Steinway Street below the Grand Central Parkway. Epstein and Billy Boyle. The coffee shop has a name, but it's written in Arabic and there's no English translation. Arab Attitude, Epstein decides. In his experience, Arabs are even more macho than Hispanics. The young ones, anyway, the ones born here. You offended them every time you opened your mouth.

Maybe this is why El-Shaer doesn't take off when Billy Boyle stops the unmarked Ford in front of the coffee house, when Billy and Epstein leave the car and walk toward him, when Billy Boyle flashes his badge.

'Turn around and put your hands behind your back.'

El-Shaer's eyes widen at Boyle's take-no-prisoners tone, but he doesn't move until Boyle spins him around. Much the smaller of the two, the Arab offers little in the way of resistance, though he does mutter something in Arabic that Epstein assumes to be unflattering. El-Shaer is Toufiq's bookkeeper. Epstein knows this because he has an unregistered snitch inside Toufiq's crew, a man named Fouad Birou.

NYPD regulations require informants to be registered as they're acquired. But this mandate is routinely ignored. First, because dozens of employees have access to the registry, employees who have, on occasion, sold the list to the bad guys. Second, because snitches on the registry are open season for other cops. OCCB, Vice, Narcotics, Major Crimes, Special Victims . . . everybody wants a pass at your snitch, which does not make for a trusting relationship. Not at all.

'Where are you taking me?'

'For a drive, Abe,' Epstein responds.

'My name is not Abe. Do I look like a Jew?'

'Ibrahim, right? Ibrahim El Shaer? So, Abraham, Ibrahim
. . . you gotta forgive me if I assumed they were the same.
Arabs and Jews being people of the book and all that.'

Billy Boyle cuffs and frisks El-Shaer before leading him
back to the Ford. Epstein trails a half-step behind. At the
last minute, he pushes onto the backseat alongside El-Shaer.

'Am I under arrest?' El-Shaer asks

Epstein hesitates, then says, 'In a manner of speaking.'

'For what crime?'

'Spittin' on the sidewalk. Do you deny the charge?'
Epstein raises a hand. 'Wait, I haven't read your constitu-
tional rights to you.' He wipes his hand across his brow.
'Be hell to pay if we lose the case over a technicality.'

Epstein proceeds to give the standard Miranda warning,
reading the text from a card he keeps in his breast pocket,
a good luck charm he's carried since earning his gold shield.
El-Shaer gets the point and shuts up. Once inside the
precinct, he'll invoke his right to counsel. Until then, better
not to say anything.

Epstein takes advantage of the quiet to phone his wife. It's
closing in on nine o'clock and he wants to reach Sofia
before she goes to sleep.

'I have to pee so bad that I'm about to explode, but I
can't find the energy to get off the couch,' she informs her
husband following a perfunctory hello. 'I feel like a beached
whale.'

Epstein has heard this complaint before and he's not
unsympathetic. But he wants a child – children, actually –
and there isn't another way to do it. He couldn't volunteer
for birthing duties even if he was of a mind to, which he
definitely is not. Epstein doesn't really understand why he
wants kids so bad. Without doubt, kids are an endless drain
on family finances, meager enough in his case, and they
let you down more often than not. Didn't Epstein let his
own mother down when he joined the cops instead of going

to college? Andrea Epstein was truly pissed when her son broke the news. And she's still pissed. Never mind his promotions, never mind his ambitions, she probably won't forgive him if he's appointed Commissioner.

'It's almost over,' Epstein encourages. 'Tell me how you feel.'

'Take a basketball, fill it with water, shove it into your abdomen. Then you'll know. By the time this is over, I'll have enough stretch marks to pass for a fucking zebra.'

Another recurring theme. Sofia's mutilated body. Epstein has always been hot for his wife and the last few weeks have been hard on him. As will, he knows, the weeks to follow.

'When are you coming home?' Sofia asks.

'I don't know, baby. This case I'm on, it's a night and day thing.'

'But you're gonna take a leave once the baby's born?' Sofia's purr masks an underlying threat. *If you don't, I'll make you wish you were dead.*

'The minute you go into labor, I'm outta here.'

Billy Boyle pulls the Ford to a stop on Shore Boulevard, a narrow two-way street wedged between Astoria Park and the East River. He puts the car in reverse and backs into a parking space beneath the massive stone tower anchoring the Queens end of the Hells Gate Railroad Bridge. Then, together, he and Epstein drag a resisting El-Shaer into the park. To Epstein, it looks as if Ibrahim has gotten the message. There will be no phone call, no lawyer, just a private conversation, him and the two cops.

'Shit,' El-Shaer says.

The night has turned cold and their footsteps crunch on the frozen grass. A hundred feet above them, a freight train makes its way through a massive arch at the top of the tower and on to the bridge. The train moves slowly, the clack of its wheels, regular as a metronome, seeming to come from a great distance.

The sound effects please Epstein, as does the deep shadow. He wants El-Shaer frightened. Fear will speed things along.

But unlike Billy Boyle, he takes no pleasure from what's about to happen. Epstein's just following orders.

Epstein watches Billy Boyle square off with El-Shaer. In his early twenties, Ibrahim is a handsome boy, with the large dark eyes of a nocturnal primate and a well-defined, aquiline nose. His mouth is sensual, the lower lip actually succulent, while his chin is as round as a plum. All in all, he reminds Epstein of a new-age Jesus, right down to the skimpy beard.

'OK, Abe . . .'

'Don't call me Abe. I'm not—'

Billy Boyle puts an end to the conversation by slamming a fist into El-Shaer's unprotected gut. El-Shaer falls backward, on to his cuffed hands. His mouth opens, as though to scream, but his lungs can produce no more than a strangled wheeze. Epstein squats down beside him.

'Now I want you to listen close, Abe, because –' Epstein glances up at Billy Boyle's lumpy face – 'well, let me just say that listening close is in your best interest. Ya see, I got a wife who's nine months pregnant, so you can understand if I wanna get home to her as soon as possible. Plus, it's gotta be twenty fuckin' degrees out here and my balls are turnin' into ice cubes.' Epstein squeezes El-Shaer's narrow shoulder. 'Bottom line, Abe, my tolerance for bullshit is real low at the moment. That's why there's not gonna be any sparring, any manipulating. You don't tell me what I wanna know, I'm skipping right to Plan B. Now, what comes into your mind when I say the name Charlie Bousejian?'

Epstein's really hoping that El-Shaer will get the message, but it's not to be. Without ever looking at Epstein, the Arab says, 'Who?'

Epstein jumps to his feet and walks off. That's the way it is with mutts, he tells himself as Billy Boyle goes to work. They have to play macho. They have to test the waters. They just can't help themselves.

Epstein turns away to enjoy the view. Before him, the East River flows south, revealing the high-rise apartment buildings lining the Upper East Side and most of the midtown office towers. Epstein recognizes the Chrysler,

Citibank and Met Life buildings, and of course the Empire
State Building, its upper stories lit with red and green flood-
lights. Christmas lights. Epstein's view is framed by the arc
of the Triborough Bridge, which runs across the far end of
the park, and by the silver-black waters of the East River.
The tide is running hard on the river. The water bucks and
rolls as Epstein imagines El-Shaer bucking and rolling
behind him. The Arab is showing heart. He doesn't scream,
only grunts occasionally, his complaints barely audible over
the incessant clack of the freight train above.

'Enough, Billy.' Epstein walks back to squat beside El-
Shaer. He waits until El-Shaer catches his breath, then says,
'Charlie Bousejian.'

'Bousejian got whacked.' Now that he's taken his lumps,
now that he's proven himself to be a man, El-Shaer can
allow himself to open up. Maybe he broke, but it was under
torture. To Epstein, this is predictable and pathetic.

'Exactly,' Epstein replies. 'And Tony Maguire, Shawn
Peterson, Nomo Terrentino? What about them? You recognize those names?'

'Dead.'

'Dead how?'

'Whacked. They got whacked.'

'And who did they work for?'

'Paulie Margarine.'

'And who do you work for?'

As El-Shaer couldn't meet Epstein's gaze before, he now
seems unable to turn away. 'I got a right not to incriminate
myself,' he whispers.

Billy Boyle cocks a fist, but Epstein waves him away.
To Billy, mutts like El-Shaer are no more than cockroaches.

'Listen up, Abe, Epstein says, 'what we're sayin' here,
between us, is strictly off the record. Given the situation, it's
never gonna see a courtroom. You can understand that, right?'

'Yeah, but—'

'But nothin'. Either you open up or I turn him loose.'
Epstein jerks a thumb in Billy Boyle's direction. 'And if
that doesn't work – swear to God – I'll put your ass in the
river.'

El-Shaer is still looking into Epstein's eyes. Looking for what, Epstein doesn't know. But then El-Shaer's mouth opens and the words flood out. 'I know what you're thinking,' he tells Epstein, 'but it's bullshit. Rachid had nothin' to do with those guys. We don't have the muscle to challenge Paulie Margarine. Not even close. Plus, there's an FBI snitch on every block in the neighborhood. You can't fuck your girlfriend without the FBI makin' a videotape. It's like a bad joke. The cops think we're the Mafia and the Feds think we're al-Quaeda. The truth is that we're barely survivin'.'

Epstein glances over his shoulder at the mention of the FBI. Just what he needs. 'Keep goin',' he says. 'Convince me.'

After a moment, El-Shaer nods to himself. 'Bousejian and them guys, they weren't earners. They were assholes, in and out of jail every other week. Paulie's main guys are still walkin' around. What I think, Paulie's cleaning house. I mean, if we wanted a war, we wouldn't start by offing these chumps. We'd use the element of surprise to get as close to the top as possible. The element of surprise is not an advantage you get twice.'

Epstein encourages El-Shaer with a wink. 'You seem to know a lot about war. Elements, strategies? I always figured it was blaze away and see who rode off into the sunset.'

But El-Shaer is set on his path. 'Rachid,' he tells Epstein, 'is not a fighter. He's smart and he never gives up once he wants something, but he's not a warrior.'

'So, your boss is a punk?'

'Let's just say he avoids confrontation. If it was up to me, there'd be a lot more pushing back.'

Epstein gives El-Shaer a little poke. 'C'mon, you're sayin' your boss is a fag, right? A pussy?'

'Well, if the shoe fits . . .' El-Shaer laughs, a short bark, then quickly sobers. 'But what I'm trying to say is that under no circumstances did we whack those guys. Not me, not Rachid. In fact, Rachid, the last time I saw him, was pissin' his pants. That's because he thinks Paulie Margarine's gonna come after him, which is just the opposite of the way you're thinkin'. There's even a rumor that Rachid already bought a one-way ticket to Casablanca, that he'll be home by New Year's.'

Epstein has heard this story before, from his snitch, Fouad Birou. It's a story he believes to be true. Still, he looks to Billy Boyle, who cocks his head and winks. They have enough to satisfy Champliss. Epstein turns back to El-Shaer. He takes a digital recorder from his pocket and holds it up for inspection. The recorder isn't running, Epstein having zero interest in a record of the crimes he's committed over the last half-hour. But El-Shaer doesn't know this.

'You're my snitch, Abe. Till prison do us part, I own your ass. You fight me, I'll send this recording to your boss. In fact, I might even drag him into the precinct and make him listen to it while I watch. Myself, I don't think he's gonna fall in love with what you had to say about him.'

Epstein doesn't turn on the light when he enters his home. Sofia is in the living room, snoring loud enough to rattle the windowpanes. Epstein shucks his loafers and tiptoes through the small foyer and into the living room beyond. To his left, Sofia lies back in a recliner, hands folded over her swollen belly. Epstein stares at her for a moment, then drops on to the couch. He feels the tension begin to leak out, a pinprick in a water balloon. Home at last.

Home is what makes it worthwhile for Epstein, sitting on the couch, contemplating his wife, the curly hair that streams over her shoulders, her button of a nose and her soft brown skin. Sofia is a third-generation Puerto Rican. Though she barely speaks Spanish, she's intensely proud of her heritage. On this night, when she awakens to find Epstein a few feet away, her eyes narrow and she smiles.

'Ayyyy, Papi,' she says, 'come to Mami, come to Mami.'

Epstein kneels beside the recliner and lowers his head to her belly. His son is awake, his little hands and feet thumping against his mother's womb. Epstein thinks again of the Macy's showroom window and the decorations inside and what he'll do with his living room on his son's first birthday.

'This kid wants out,' Epstein says, more to himself than Sofia.

'You think so?' Sofia runs her fingers through her husband's hair. 'I think maybe he's a little genius. Maybe he's figured out that he's a lot safer where he is.'

Epstein responds by kissing Sofia. That life is filled with danger, unexpected and undeserved, is not a subject that an emergency-room nurse and her cop husband need discuss.

'You think you can make it to bed?' Epstein asks.

Sofia grasps Epstein's hands and allows him to pull her to her feet. They embrace momentarily before staggering, arm in arm, into the bedroom. Gingerly, Sofia lowers herself to the bed and rolls onto her side.

'*Por favor*,' she says.

Epstein lifts his wife's t-shirt and begins to massage the small of her back, gently at first, then with greater force. Sofia grunts appreciatively.

'You know, I felt pretty good today,' she admits. 'I was worried before, but now I know everything's gonna be OK.'

Epstein undresses quickly, then climbs into bed, spooning himself into his wife. He puts his arm around her waist, his hand coming to rest on her belly. A few minutes later, they're both asleep.

Seven

Paulie Margarine has a thing about submission and he's had it for as long as he can remember. As a kid, he was barely under control. Even the nuns and priests at St Agnes's, try as they might, never brought him to heel. How many times had his old man been called to the principal's office? Giaco Marginella was a second-generation American. His family values were definitely conservative and he had heavy hands, which he didn't hesitate to use. But Paulie wouldn't bend. And even later, when he grew up enough to admit that nobody's invincible and there are times when you have to eat shit, it wasn't fear that moved him. It was experience.

Still, he's never become resigned, never once submitted without wanting to drive his fist into somebody's mouth, as he now wants to drive his fist into the mouth of the corrections officer who frisks him. Forget the fact that he's fifty-nine years old and his knees are ancient history. Paulie hates everything about the guard. He hates the man's dismissive blue eyes, his lipless mouth, his watermelon gut, his fat little fingers. Which, incidentally, come close enough to the family jewels to produce an involuntary flinch.

'Awright,' the guard announces. 'You can go in.'

Paulie walks into the visiting room. He's been here so often he can map the layout in his head: linoleum floors, green tile walls and a white plaster ceiling, Formica tables and plastic chairs scattered about. Good hard surfaces that reflect noise the way a mirror reflects light. You get enough conversations going and it sounds like you stuck your head in a beehive. Paulie's hearing isn't getting better as he ages, far from it. There are times, especially on weekends and holidays, when he can't understand a word Freddy says.

Freddy Marginella is Paulie's youngest child. He's sitting at a table at the far end of the room with his back to the wall. Paulie catches his son's eye and nods once before making his way around the tables that dot the room. His knees are killing him, but he doesn't limp. Concealment is a way of life for Paulie. You never tell anybody more than he has to know, not even your own kid. And you especially hide weakness.

Paulie slides into a seat across from his boy. He folds his hands on the tabletop and says, 'What's new?'

'Poetry,' Freddy responds. 'I'm takin' a poetry class.'

At twenty-five, Freddy is tall and beefy. Like his father, he's a man of casual strength, with a wide face and high cheekbones that mask incipient jowls. Dark circles beneath his eyes make him look older than his years.

'Haiku poetry,' Freddy continues. 'Japanese, three lines.'

Paulie encourages his son with a nod, though he has no idea what the kid's talking about. 'Yeah, and?'

'And nothin'. I'll be up for parole in a year, so I'm workin' on a package for the board.'

'You figure brown-nosin' some fag poetry teacher is gonna impress a parole board?'

'Hey, Pop, you wanna hear my poem or what?'

'Sure, go ahead.'

Freddy drops his elbows to the table and leans forward, his voice dropping to a whisper: 'Pink light from a street-lamp/the shadow of rat in a trash can/broken teeth clatter on the sidewalk. Pay up, mother-fucker.'

Paulie tries to hold it in, but he can't help himself. He laughs until tears pour from his eyes. That's the good news about Freddy Marginella. He's got a sense of humor and everyone likes him. Paulie knows that times have changed and success is more about persuasion than fear. Paulie's two older children, Mike and Rebecca, are both successes. Mike's an accountant with an MBA, Rebecca a tax attorney. They live on the other side of the continent, as far from their old man's criminal activities as possible. Neither has been home for a holiday, any holiday, since their mother passed eight years before. That would be Marie the Martyr.

Freddy is Paulie Margarine's last, best chance. Paulie wants to back off, to retire without jeopardizing his income. His associates would never stand for that. For them, you're either in the life, sharing the work and the risks, or you're out. There are no free rides. On the other hand, a son who needs schooling might be persuaded to accept a moderate piece of the action in return for benefits to come.

Paulie wipes his eyes. 'That's four lines,' he observes.

'What?'

'The poem, it sounded like four lines, not three.'

'Naw, the last line is actually the title.'

'Then why didn't you say it first?'

'I didn't wanna ruin the punch line.'

Paulie consider this for a moment before changing the subject, 'You hear about Tony?'

'Yeah, it's all over the news. You think it was the raghead?'

'If you asked me before all this started, I would've said Rachid Toufiq doesn't have the organization or the balls. I mean, he was distributing powder for me in Arab neighborhoods. Still is for that matter, because the ragheads only buy from each other. But it's gotta be somebody took Tony out, and the rest of 'em, too. They didn't commit fuckin' suicide. Besides, the way it's shapin' up, I'm gonna look weak if I don't make a move, and soon. Nobody's gonna pay me protection if I can't protect myself.'

Deep down, Paulie Margarine admires his son. Yeah, Freddy did something stupid. In fact, two somethings. He tried to pull off an armed robbery with no planning and he chose a partner with the intelligence and mentality of a starving reptile. No surprise that a clerk got roughed up pretty bad and Freddy was collared at the scene. And no surprise that Freddy drew five years, even with no record. But Freddy stood up. That's the good news. He never whined and he still doesn't whine. The screws, the food, the other cons? What Freddy tells his old man is that he just wants to do his time and get out.

Paulie's driving his Caddy south on the Thruway, taking his time in the middle lane, ignoring the traffic around him.

On the stereo, Sam Cook launches into *You Send Me*. As Paulie hums along, his thoughts are mostly of his son and not the hard decisions he'll soon have to make. Against all odds, he feels relaxed and confident.

Or maybe not. When the cell phone tucked beneath the Caddy's front seat blares the opening notes of the *William Tell Overture*, Paulie jumps so high the top his head pounds into the roof hard enough raise a bruise. Despite the blow, his mind leaps into high gear, thoughts ripping back and forth like bullets against the walls of a cave. Possibilities are thrown up, explanations galore, none of which he can stop long enough to examine. But Paulie Margarine's sure of one thing: that's not his fucking cell phone playing *The Lone Ranger* theme song.

Paulie keeps his eyes on the road while he fumbles beneath the seat. The *William Tell Overture* continues to sound, the volume so high all he can think about is shutting it off. But when he finally scoops up the phone, he doesn't do anything for a minute. Just holds it up and stares at the little screen: 'PRIVATE NAME/PRIVATE NUMBER'.

His first instinct is to heave the device out the window. Dump the phone, frustrate whoever's on the other end, make him show his face if he wants to communicate. One thing certain, the prick wants him to answer.

But Paulie has to know. He has to know who's on the other end, who planted a phone in his car when he might have planted a bomb. Until the cell phone began to ring, Paulie had no idea anybody had been near the Caddy. The Caddy that's been sitting in his garage for the last three days, locked and alarmed.

Paulie answers the phone, his eyes moving to the car's mirrors. 'Who the fuck is this?' he growls.

'This is the man who killed Tony Maguire, Shawn Peterson, Nomo Terrentino and Charlie Bousejian. You can call me Thorpe.'

Stunned doesn't begin to describe Paulie's reaction. The voice on the other end of the line is precise, not to mention confident, not to mention fucking amused. This is a man

Paulie will kill at the earliest opportunity. This is a man Paulie
will wait twenty years to kill. He will pass the responsibility
for killing this man to his son and his grandson.

'I realize this must come as a bit of a shock, my calling
out of nowhere. But we needed to communicate over a
secure line and I couldn't see how else to accomplish that.
As it is, what we say is being encrypted on one end and
decrypted on the other.'

Paulie takes a deep breath. The man has a slight accent,
though Paulie can't place it exactly. England, he's thinking,
or Ireland. Not a voice, anyway, that Paulie's heard before.

'I'm gonna cut your balls off,' he says. 'I'm gonna find
you and cut your balls off. I'm gonna do it myself.'

'No, you're not. And that's the essential point. You're not
going to find me. You have no way to find me. I can damage
your interests with virtually no risk to my own. Once you
accept this, we'll be on the way to concluding our business.'

'You and me, scumbag, we got no business.'

'Oh, yes, we do, Paulie. Tony Maguire and the rest were
all second rate and we both know it. So far, I've only pruned
a few dying branches from the family tree. That will change
abruptly unless we come to an understanding. I know I lack
your talent for threatening speech. I tend to put my thoughts
simply. But I don't make threats I can't keep. You'll simply
have to pay up.'

'Pay up?'

'Now, I know you're a stubborn man. As I know you're
a proud man. I know, also, how the extortion game works.
I know that sometimes the mark doesn't pay, despite the
consequences. That's all right with me. I'm content to be
certain that you won't run to the police. Nevertheless, you
should understand this. For the present, I'm content to
disrupt your operations. But if I'm forced to roll up my
blanket and move on, without doubt I'll kill you before I
go. And by the way, how's Freddy?'

Paulie registers the threats, but doesn't react. Instead,
he hangs up. He half expects the phone to ring again. The
William Tell Overture, all those trumpets. As a kid, he

must've watched a thousand episodes of *The Lone Ranger*, hoping the masked asshole would get blown away. No such luck.

The phone remains silent and Paulie's attention gradually returns to the road. He's coming up on the tollbooths for the Triborough Bridge and he automatically seeks out the least-crowded EZ-PASS lane. He'll have to go underground now, him and everyone else in his crew. That's a no-brainer. But what will he tell them? Forget what the FBI says, Paulie Margarine isn't Adolph Hitler. He can't just order his men to hide in their homes until further notice. He has to tell them why they can't show their faces on the street. And that means war. That means he'll have to blame Toufiq, have to launch a counterattack. To buy time, if for no other reason.

Paulie rolls through the toll plaza and accelerates on to the bridge. He's outwardly calm, having swallowed his rage. Not that the fire has been extinguished. Paulie's anger is a smoldering lump of coal burning somewhere in his gut. Extortion? Pay up? Thorpe might as well have said, 'Bend over and spread 'em.'

The Triborough Bridge provides a breathtaking view of the East River and Manhattan skyline, especially on winter afternoons when the breeze is up. But Paulie's mind is elsewhere. He's wondering how Thorpe knows so much about Paulie Margarine's business. How he knows where Paulie parks his car, knows about Freddy, even when Paulie's gonna visit. And that's the key. That's Thorpe's Achilles' heel. Who knew what and when did he know it?

Eight

First thing, after Carter hits the bathroom the following morning, he plunks down in front of his computer, enters his password, and reviews three news stories on the Macy's Massacre, one from each of New York's major newspapers. He doesn't have to read every word. The headlines, by themselves, provide enough information. Tony Maguire's brain isn't functioning and it's never going to function. According to an unnamed source inside Bellevue Hospital, one who's apparently spoken to every reporter in town, Maguire will be officially and forever dead a few seconds after his family agrees to pull the plug. Good news, indeed.

Carter fires off an e-mail to Thorpe, arguing that the mark is deceased by any meaningful definition of the word, and that he, Carter, is entitled to compensation for his work. For good measure, he attaches the newspaper stories to the e-mail.

Initially disheartened to find the mark alive in any sense of the word, Carter now believes that his thrust was accurate. His mistake was in not removing the knife. The blade had intersected the descending aorta, as it was meant to do, but the blade also acted as a plug, limiting blood loss. Not totally, of course, but the paramedics must have detected faint signs of life when they arrived. Enough life to justify shoving a tube down the mark's throat and needles into his arms, to deliver fluids sufficient to maintain his blood pressure, to force oxygen into his lungs. Carter is familiar with battlefield medicine. He's only glad the medics didn't arrive sooner. If there was any hope of recovery, no matter how long term, he'd never get paid.

Carter leaves the computer running while he chows down

a bowl of cereal topped with a slightly overripe banana. This is the last banana of a bunch he purchased five days before and Carter is happy to eat it. Usually, he has to throw the last banana out. Carter dislikes waste as much as he loves precision. To him, they're opposite sides of the same coin.

Thorpe has not replied by the time Carter finishes washing the dishes and Carter turns off the computer before heading out to the gym. He's not crazy about the gym. Too many people. But Carter's pretty much a fitness fanatic. When he crossed the African continent a couple of years ago, a sack of diamonds strapped to the inside of his thigh, fitness saved him. He'd been one small step ahead of the men he and his partner stole the diamonds from, the men who stole them from somebody else, who stole them from somebody else.

In Sierra Leone, theft was a train with a caboose, the natives who worked the mines. No more than slaves, they toiled at the point of a gun, barely fed, knee-deep in muck from sunrise to sunset. On occasion, the boy soldiers mowed them down for the fun of it.

Maybe, Carter decides as he steps on to a treadmill and starts it up, the diamonds are owned by the earth. Maybe the trouble starts when they're stolen from the earth, one thief chasing another until the polished stones finally rest on some rich whore's cleavage. Until the ultimate responsibility rests on the shoulders of the ultimate thief.

There's a muted, hi-def TV set on the mirrored wall in front of the treadmills, exercise bikes and stair climbers, tuned to the Jerry Springer Show. Carter watches for a moment, then steps up the pace. Predictably, he's disgusted. A morbidly obese white woman confronting a morbidly obese Latina over a morbidly obese love interest. Their words run across the face of the monitor.

Yeah, ya bleep, I bleeped your bleeping boyfriend.

I'll kill you, you bleeping bleeper.

The combatants continue the debate for another thirty seconds before Jerry introduces a second male, this one short and squat, his hair greasy enough to ignite. His name is Jeff and he struts on to the raised platform.

Yeah, ya bleep, he tells the first male, *I bleeped your girl-friend and she begged for more.*

Then they're all fighting, the girls and the boys, revealing their essential mediocrity with each clumsy punch, each round-house, open-handed slap. Carter decides that he could slaughter the lot, even without a weapon, in under a minute. And he'd be more than happy to perform the task.

After a moment, Jerry's muscle-bound crew pulls the combatants apart. The short man with the greasy hair is bleeding from a long scratch beneath his ear. The morbidly-obese white woman has had her wig yanked away, revealing a head of thin yellow hair that barely covers her scalp. They really shout at each other now, the bleeps overlapping, the subtitles barely able to keep up.

Carter turns his head away. In the course of his short life, he's witnessed unspeakable savagery without flinching. Worse, he's committed acts so awful that he thinks himself past even the hope of redemption. But for all the blood, Carter has never willingly surrendered his dignity. Nor did the most hapless of his victims, the boy soldiers who barely understood the concept of profit and loss. Sure, they begged. They screamed and cried and shit their pants, too. That didn't make them less than human, not in Carter's eyes. Not like these degraded fools.

Carter imagines the obese Latina, years from now, playing the tape for her grandchildren. *See, I was on television. I was famous once. Admire me.*

'Jerry, he motivates me.'

The voice comes from Carter's left and he turns to discover a stunning young blonde. The blonde wears a spandex body suit, blue and red, the colors at a diagonal, so that arms and opposite legs match.

'Pardon?' he says.

'I use Jerry for inspiration.' The girl smiles, exposing a set of brilliant porcelain veneers. 'See, they're everything I don't want to be. The whole bunch. Jerry, too.'

Carter believes he's being hit on, and not for the first time at this gym. Though there's nothing memorable about his face, Carter's not a bad-looking man. True, his eyes are a little too close together, his mouth on the narrow side, his chin somewhat soft. But nothing major. Just a regular guy, until you looked into his eyes.

Carter's eyes are blue and flat. They're as dead as his soul and he knows it. But the girl isn't looking into his eyes. She's glancing, from time to time, at his body. Fully clothed, Carter may not impress, may even appear harmless, but now his flesh ripples over his skeleton as he paces off a six-minute mile, his thighs and calves especially.

'How long does it take?' Carter asks.

'Before what?'

'Before you internalize the lesson and switch to another show.'

The woman looks at him for a moment, her face reddening, then turns away. She's insulted, obviously, though Carter meant no offense. He was just curious. But Carter tends to say the wrong thing. All that time alone before Janie saved him? He never learned the rules. Never learned the subtleties of give and take.

His workout concluded, Carter hops on the 19A bus running along Twenty-First Street into Long Island City. He exits at Thirty-Eighth Avenue and walks three blocks to a rented garage where he picks up his van. From there, he heads into Manhattan, via the Fifty-Ninth Street Bridge, to his final destination, the Cabrini Nursing Center. Carter's in a good mood, and so is Janie, whose eyes sparkle when he enters her room at eleven thirty. The nurses have Janie sitting in a recliner and Carter settles on the edge of her bed.

'I have to work late tonight, so I took the morning off,' he explains.

Blink.

'Everything going all right?'

Blink.

Carter leans closer. He smiles. 'Are you stoned? Did you get morphine this morning?'

Blink.

'I thought as much.' Carter wishes his mock-frown could

draw a smile he can only imagine. The joke is that Janie was as straight as they come before her illness, an anti-drug zealot. 'I met a girl this morning. At the gym.'

Carter continues, embellishing freely as he describes Jerry Springer's repugnant guests. In this version, the girl on the treadmill next to him defends the show. Carter's problem, she explains, is that he takes the mayhem, most of which is staged, way too seriously.

'Do you know what I finally said to her?'

Blink, blink.

'I told her that some men are born without souls and that some have their souls burned away. But what kind of man – or woman, for that matter – uses his soul for toilet paper? Janie, the girl was a real knockout, but I blew any chance I had right there. She thought I was talking about her.'

Blink.

Carter grins. 'OK, I admit it. I probably was talking about her. But if degradation amuses her . . . I mean, what's the point? We're not goin' anywhere.'

Blink.

Another smile from Carter. His propensity for driving women away has been an issue since he was an adolescent. 'You want me to read for a while?'

Blink.

Carter takes the bible from a drawer and opens it to Proverbs. He begins where he left off on the night before.

'The Lord possessed me in the beginning of his ways, before he made anything from the beginning. I was set up from eternity, and of old before the earth was made. The depths were not as yet, and I was already conceived, neither had the fountains of waters as yet sprung out. The mountains had not yet been established; before the hills I was brought forth. He had not yet made the earth, nor the rivers, nor the poles of the world. When he prepared the heavens, I was present; when he enclosed the depths; when he established the sky above, and poised the fountains of waters; when he compassed the sea with its bounds, and set a law to the waters that they should not pass their limits; when he balanced the foundations of the earth. I was with him forming all things.'

Carter shakes his head. There are times when the desire to retrieve his life overwhelms him. When he wishes there was a redo button in his brain like the one on his computer. Janie was too young to care for him when their mother died. So the state, in its wisdom, shipped him off to the Abernathys' farm. Foster parents, that's what the social worker called David and Lucille. But the Abernathys were managers, not parents. Middle-aged, their lives were guided solely by profit and loss. This was as true of Carter as it was of the corn in their fields, or the pigs or the chickens. The Abernathys received a check each month from the Indiana Department of Human Services for $212. 65. Every expense was weighed against that sum, the food on his plate, his shoes and socks, the laundry detergent to clean his clothes, the oil burned to heat his room. Lest he rip his clothes in play, or even soil them, Carter was confined to the home after school. Lest he wear out his shoes, he was required to go barefoot indoors. And when the social worker paid a visit every month or so, he was compelled to express gratitude for the Abernathys' largesse.

Eventually, four years later, when she turned eighteen, Janie came for her brother. Too late, of course, way too late, but she did come.

Carter looks up to find his sister asleep. Just as well, for he has things to do. He stands, approaches her chair, bends over to bestow a kiss on her forehead. She did come, he tells himself. She might have abandoned me, but she came.

'Bye, honey. See ya tomorrow.'

Nine

Carter drives back to Astoria and parks the van on Thirty-First Street beneath the el. As plain as Carter on the outside, the van's interior has been impressively tricked out. There's no bling, of course. A metal floor running from the front seat to the back doors, a pair of sliding windows toward the rear, empty boxes stacked one atop the other. The van is designed not to push buttons, especially those of cops. Your paperwork's in order, here's your ticket, so long.

Carter slips off a panel on the driver's side of the van to reveal a number of weapons, among them a sniper rifle he first used in Iraq, an XM25. Little more than a customized version of the M14, standard issue before Vietnam, the XM25 is a semi-automatic weapon and not prized by sharp-shooters. Bolt-action is all the rage now, one shot, then reload. But Carter's willing to sacrifice a little accuracy for the fifty-round magazine he jams into the gun's underbelly. Sniping is all about stealth, the basic idea to shoot without being seen, a goal Carter embraces wholeheartedly. But ideas are not realities and goals are only goals, so Carter is prepared to exercise plan B if the shit hits the fan. He's prepared to shoot his way out.

Carter arranges the boxes in two stacks, separated by a single box just high enough to support the rifle's biped. His line of sight, through an open rear window, is of the far side of the street to a distance of approximately 300 meters.

Carter is wearing a navy-blue jacket over a black turtle-neck sweater and thin black gloves. He completes this outfit by donning a nylon ski mask, also black. Finally, he peers through the rifle's Unerti 10X scope. The front door of

Sweet's Bar and Grill jumps into view, disappears as an oncoming truck goes by, appears again just as suddenly.

Traffic, a hazard for which Carter, who's conducted several practice runs, is prepared. He can see oncoming vehicles, at least until he sights down on a target, but not vehicles coming from behind him. These he has to hear.

Carter likes a challenge, likes overcoming obstacles, and he's reached the point when he can differentiate between busses and large trucks, SUVs and sedans by the hum of their tires on the asphalt and the pitch of their engines. More importantly, he's learned to gauge the speed of these vehicles well enough to estimate the number of seconds before they intersect his line of sight. Except, of course, when a train passes overhead.

While he waits for a target to appear, Carter tracks the vehicles on both sides of the road. Patience is another aspect of the sniper's art, like stealth. You acquire a position first, then you make yourself invisible until a target presents itself. Your goal is to maintain focus, no matter how long it takes. But Carter's mind soon begins to drift.

More slippage.

Eventually, Carter's thoughts settle on Montgomery Thorpe, who claimed, when he and Carter first met, to be an Australian educated at Sandhurst, Britain's Royal Military Academy. Carter was initially skeptical, as well he should have been. The mercenary scene was chock full of braggarts and blowhards. But then one night, as they ripped through the countryside in an armored Humvee, Thorpe delivered an extremely detailed monologue on Roman military tactics and how they were eventually overcome by far more primitive societies.

'Throughout history,' he concluded, 'every advance in weaponry, tactics and strategy has resulted in the formation of a successful counter. The trick is to be nimble.' As the months went by, Thorpe occasionally added to this bottom line by analyzing the collapse of other great militaries, the Ottomans in the near east, Napoleon in Europe, the Ashanti in Africa.

They were in Iraq, Carter and Thorpe, when these lectures

took place, working for Coldstream Military Operations. Their little mercenary band had devolved into a virtual hit squad by then. Worse still, they no longer knew who they worked for. A Russian oligarch, as one rumor had it? Or a Saudi oil prince? Or the CIA? Or what was left of the KGB? Or the Chinese? All Carter knew was that the money was good, twice what Halliburton's people got. All Carter knew was that when he finally went home, he wouldn't be sporting empty pockets.

But then Coldstream went bust and the administrators vanished without a trace. And there was no money. And it was off to Africa.

Two years later, when Thorpe found him again, Carter was in Dar es Salaam, at the Sea Cliff Hotel, relaxing by the pool after dinner. They'd shared a pleasant drink, reliving old times, then taken a little stroll by the cliff. The setting was magnificent. The sun was dropping into the Pacific Ocean and the dhows' triangular sails were smoldering orange triangles, the color made all the more intense by the darkening seas.

Thorpe had chosen the moment of his approach carefully. Carter wasn't exactly penniless, but the blood diamonds he'd carried across the continent hadn't fetched the price he'd hoped for. Plus, he had to wonder exactly what he'd do when he got back to the States. Carter had stumbled through high school, barely earning a diploma, then joined the army a month later. And what had the army taught him, except to kill?

Thorpe invoked this unpleasant truth as they walked. Character is destiny, he insisted, and aptitude is aptitude. Delta Force hadn't perverted Lenny Carter. Far from it. The military and Carter were a perfect fit. And what Carter must now do, with a military career off the table, is market his talents and training on the free market. Not some imagined set of skills he doesn't have, but the ones he actually does.

That said, they strolled in silence for a time. Carter was being pitched, pitched by a master, and he knew it. He didn't object. Sooner or later, a bottom line would appear.

Thorpe always had a bottom line. As he had a talent for pushing the right buttons at the tight time.

Vulnerabilities, niche markets and entrepreneurship were the subject of Thorpe's second lecture. Because they work outside the law, he began, criminal enterprises rapidly accumulate capital. Because they cannot turn to the police when faced with aggression, they must protect their capital with ferociously-applied force. But of what use is force against an aggressor who can't be found? The answer, Thorpe explained, is none: an anonymous assassin, motivated by financial gain and therefore presumably rational, has every advantage. Naturally, the mark will resist this conclusion, not least because the situation is entirely novel. But the heads of criminal enterprises are also rational actors. They will sue for peace once they internalize their helplessness.

Carter waited until he was sure Thorpe was finished, then asked, 'How much?'

'Per head?'

'Yeah.'

'Twenty grand.'

The door to Sweet's Bar and Grill opens suddenly and a man staggers out to light a cigarette. A second later, he's joined by a woman. Carter brings his eyes to the rifle's scope and sights down on the man. Not a mark.

Sweet's is nominally owned by an aging alcoholic named Harry Sweets, but Paulie Margarine has a controlling interest in the bar, as he does in several legit businesses. Sweets is also where Paulie holds court, his minions coming and going. According to Thorpe, Paulie has been powerfully influenced by John Gotti, who delivered sensitive instructions to his people vis-à-vis walk-and-talks outside his social club. Paulie, who doesn't trust phones any more than did the Dapper Don, has added a little fillip to the walk-and-talk. His strolls take place beneath the el as trains pass overhead.

According to Thorpe, any tactic, when analyzed, will yield a vulnerability, a sacrifice of one benefit to achieve another. True, Paulie's tactic will most likely frustrate the cops and their long-distance microphones. Not so an assassin.

Carter's wait drags on for another hour. He doesn't mind. Alone in the shadows, he feels at home, as if designed for the environment. Outside, the sidewalks are busy, as are the stairways leading up to the el. Christmas is coming and there's a tension in the air that Carter, from a distance, finds pleasant. The children are especially exuberant. They skip down the street, blowing little clouds of steam into the frigid air. As he watches, Carter's eyes drift along the sidewalk, restless as the wind-blown litter. Eventually, his gaze settles on a panhandler huddled against the wall of a Dunkin' Donuts. The panhandler is little more than a bundle of rags and he sits unmoving, despite the cold. Very occasionally, someone pauses long enough to give up some spare change and Carter imagines the little clink of coin on coin. The panhandler himself appears not to notice.

A young girl, her head rising barely to her father's hip, stops before the beggar. She stares at the man for a moment, then yanks on her father's hand. Carter is too far away to make out her features, but he imagines her lips moving rapidly as she looks up at her dad, who wants only to be home, to be done with the day's obligations. His free hand clutches a pair of shopping bags and his shoulders sag with fatigue. He stops nevertheless, dropping his packages to the sidewalk as he digs beneath his coat for a suitable offering. Finally, he comes up with a bill, which he hands to his daughter. Suddenly shy, she edges toward the panhandler, looking back at her father for reassurance before dropping the bill into his cup. The panhandler remains motionless throughout.

Carter is wondering what it's like to be homeless four days before Christmas. Does the man recall happier times, perhaps his own childhood? Carter remembers being astounded on that first Christmas with Janie. The tree, the brilliant Christmas wrappings, the presents. At first, his senses were overwhelmed and he smelled a trap of some kind. But then he dug in, happier at that moment than he'd ever been in his life.

The door to Sweet's opens and Paulie Margarine steps out, shortly followed by Angelo 'Bruno' Brunale, one of his closest advisors. Carter doesn't see them exit, his eyes only coming to them as they stand together on the sidewalk. More slippage? Carter drops his eyes to the scope and focuses on Brunale, ignoring the traffic. He recognizes the man from a file in his computer that includes shots of Paulie Margarine's family among its two dozen photographs. Brunale is a suitable target for this phase of the operation.

Carter settles back on his heels as a train approaches. He draws a long breath through his nose, then exhales slowly through his mouth, draining the tension. He half expects Paulie and his lieutenant to go back inside, but they remain on the sidewalk after the train passes. As Carter waits for an opening in the traffic, he finds himself thinking about Angelo Brunale's upcoming Christmas. He envisions a Christmas tree, children and grandchildren, a faithful dog curled before a smoldering fire, Christmas dinner roasting in the oven. Then Carter remembers another of Thorpe's many maxims. No predator can afford to feel sorry for its prey.

Ten

Epstein sits at his desk at the Organized Crime Control Bureau, lost in his work. It's eight o'clock in the morning, twelve hours before Bruno Brunale's execution. An hour hence, Epstein will report to his boss, Inspector Champliss, and to the inspector's boss, Deputy Chief Radisson. As Radisson has a hair-trigger temper and a penchant for humiliating his inferiors (including Champliss), Epstein ordinarily dreads these meetings. But not this time. This time the fates have delivered a trio of Christmas miracles.

Almost as an afterthought, Epstein had instructed Billy Boyle to check surveillance cameras at subways stations up and down Seventh Avenue. The task was one of those hoops you had to jump through lest the bosses ask you why you didn't, and no positive outcome was anticipated. But the man hours have paid off. Against all odds, Epstein's detectives have uncovered a tape of Tony Maguire's killer, his floppy hat in place, exiting the subway station at Columbus Circle. This is a lead by any definition of the word and the bosses will almost certainly be grateful, despite the grainy images being (miracle number two) useless for purposes of identification.

Epstein's third miracle is of lesser significance – an interesting fact, if true, but one likely to lead nowhere, what with the absence of evidence not being evidence. While inside Macy's, the perpetrator appeared to rest his fingers on a glass display case. Certainly, his fingertips had come within millimeters of it. Yet despite their best efforts, which included superglue fuming, the lab rats were unable to raise his prints. Sergeant Tina Metzenbaum, a long-time CSU supervisor with whom Epstein has been flirting for years, had called him only ten minutes before.

'What I think,' she told Epstein, 'is that our boy's a non-secretor.'

As both knew, non-secretor, when applied to fingerprint identification, refers to individuals who don't sweat. Not sweating, they fail to excrete the oils necessary to produce a latent print. But the percentage of non-secretors in the general population is tiny. When Epstein later reviewed the video, it seemed just as likely that the perp never touched the glass.

'I thought CSU was able to recover prints from non-secretors?'

'Well, that's just it, Solly. When I examined the glass under a microscope, I saw a very faint smudge. At least I think I did.'

That's good enough for Epstein and he will present this opinion to his bosses as if it was a precious jewel.

The command performance takes place in OCCB's gigantic media room. Tape recorders, digital and film cameras of every description, bugging and tracking devices, computers programmed to enhance images and remove ambient noise from audio tapes. Called The Black Hole, into which stray bits of evidence are sucked, never to be seen again, the room is a maze of equipment benches, electric lines and cables. The arrangement has an organic feel to it, new devices having been randomly grafted to the mix as the various technologies developed. The big difference is the odor, in this case of dust and ozone, not trees and grass.

Epstein was a year mastering the terrain. No big deal, because efficiency is purely optional at OCCB. The Bureau is all about the slow pace of its multi-year investigations, about the tedious accumulation of evidence. This is an assignment that calls for a stubborn attitude, along with the stamina of a canoeist paddling upstream. The basic aim is to generate enormous headlines by indicting whole organizations, from top to bottom. In another room on another floor, uncounted hours of audio and video, captured on DVDs, CDs or tape, rest on metal shelves.

Their current investigation, propelled as it is by the fear of a gang war, is the anomaly. Epstein doesn't know why the case was given to OCCB and he probably never will. They'd been following the string of assassinations from a distance, as they were following the activities of two dozen other criminal enterprises. Then, out of nowhere, careers were on the line. Was that good for him and Billy Boyle? On the one hand, Epstein has some measure of control. On the other, his failure to produce a suspect might negatively impact his outsized ambitions.

As his old man might've said, if he'd hung around long enough, Oy, vey, I'm lucky I got my ears.

Epstein begins the show with a simple playback, the various snippets of video tracking Carter's sixteen minutes inside Macy's having been spliced together overnight. This is the first time either of his superiors has seen the tape in any form and they're clearly fascinated. All to the good.

Six minutes later, Epstein stops the tape with the subject kneeling before a glass display case. 'CSU thinks he actually touched the glass. The reason he didn't leave prints is because he's a non-secretor.'

This isn't entirely true. Sergeant Tina Metzenbaum does not speak for the Crime Scene Unit. But Epstein is pleased when a lively discussion between Champliss and Radisson follows, a discussion in which Radisson confuses non-secretor, as it applies to the analysis of bodily fluids, with the term as it applies to fingerprint analysis. Epstein thinks that Champliss would like to correct his superior but doesn't have the balls. Large enough to dominate a room, Radisson commonly reverts to a ferocious glare if challenged, especially when he's wrong.

'How do you identify a non-secretor if you come across one?' Radisson finally asks.

Epstein replies first. 'Put him in the box with Billy Boyle and see if he sweats.'

After an exchange of manly chuckles, Epstein restarts the tape and they watch in silence until Carter finally disappears into the subway. Then Epstein leads them to another machine and punches the play button. He speaks over the running tape.

'This footage was captured by a token booth camera at the Columbus Circle station. Though his face remains hidden, we definitely see the perp walking toward an exit leading to Broadway. Right now, I have two men working the street, checking out surveillance cameras in stores and in the hotels on Central Park South. I can spare a couple more if you want to go that way.'

'What I want,' Radisson declares, 'is for this not to escalate.'

Epstein wants to tell Radisson not to hold his breath. Backed into a corner, Paulie Margarine will have to react. But Champliss isn't the only one intimidated by Radisson's temper.

'I hope to have something on that by tomorrow morning,' he says.

Radisson nods once and Champliss positively beams. They will not have to face the press empty-handed. Champliss looks up at his boss.

'The non-secretor business, should we call the evidence seriological or biological?' he asks.

Sofia is seated on the couch when Epstein walks through the door of his modest home in Bay Ridge a bit before noon. She has a pillow clutched to her belly, watching a History Channel documentary about the potential for catastrophic tsunamis on the east coast of the United States. The baby is wide awake and restless; his kicks and thrusts make little eruptions on Sofia's abdomen, leading them to exchange the usual joke about Jonathon being a space alien about to claw his way out of the womb. Then Epstein sits alongside his wife and takes her into his arms.

They remain that way for some time, listening to each other breathe, watching giant waves rip through Manhattan's skyline. In fact, as Epstein knows, to reach Manhattan, the tsunami would have to pass over Brooklyn. But Epstein isn't bothered by predictions of doom. He's a relentlessly optimistic man, undaunted by the cop experience, a man not given to questioning his choices, especially his choice of the woman sitting next to him. He's only sure that he has to have her.

'How come,' Sofia asks, 'you always know what I need?'

Epstein thinks for a minute before saying, 'You've got to think that way, think about what people need. You have to take care of the people you care for.'

'Is that the way you're gonna think about our son?'

'Yeah, what he needs, not necessarily what he wants.' Epstein leans over to plant a kiss on Sofia's left cheek. 'But what I really think is there's no right way to raise a kid. There's better ways and worse ways, but it's mostly a crap-shoot.'

Sofia considers this for a moment, then says, 'If I don't have the baby first, I want you to take me to midnight mass on Christmas Eve. I don't give a damn if you have to take me in a wheelchair. I want to go.'

'To St Patrick's Cathedral?' Epstein asks. 'In Manhattan?'

'Yeah.'

Epstein's first impulse is to reject Sofia's request out of hand. The logistics, the crowds, the possibility that she'll go into labor during the Offertory? Fuck it. But Epstein ignores this impulse. To his thinking, problems are to be solved, not dismissed. Sofia is a religious, not to mention superstitious, woman. He knew that when he married her.

First thing, he'll have to park in a bus stop, there being no other possibility on that section of Fifth Avenue. That means using his 'ON OFFICAL POLICE BUSINESS' placard, a technical violation but one likely to go unpunished on Christmas Eve. And there's his aunt Marie, who was confined to a wheelchair before her death. Most likely her son, Andy, has the wheelchair stored in his garage. Andy's a pack rat. He has trouble throwing out coffee grinds. And as for Sofia going into labor? While still a rookie patrol officer, Epstein delivered twins girls in a Lower East Side tenement. If necessary, he'll deliver Jonathon himself.

'Consider it done,' he tells his wife.

*   *   *

Billy Boyle picks Epstein up an hour later and they drive
to a strip mall on Route 4 in New Jersey. The wrong strip
mall, as it turns out. There's no Italian restaurant among
its dozen businesses. Epstein tells Billy Boyle to drive on,
try the next one. Instead, Boyle uses his cell phone to call
information. He asks for the phone number of Villa Napoli
in Teaneck, then calls the restaurant for directions. Epstein's
annoyed, but says nothing. Much more than rabbi and under-
ling, he and Billy Boyle are in it for the long run. Epstein
has already taken the captain's exam and he's certain he
aced the test. Just as he's certain that when he moves up,
Billy Boyle will come along. Even if Epstein has to call in
every favor he's ever granted.

Ten minutes later, they walk into Villa Napoli to find
Dave Flannery already eating. Flannery is hugely overweight
and he sits with his chair pulled away from the table to
leave room for his gut. Epstein looks over at Billy Boyle's
lumpy face. The man's slash of a mouth is pulled into a
predictable grimace. Boyle prides himself on his flat belly
and broad shoulders. On his self-discipline, too.

'Be cool, little brother,' Epstein advises.

Billy Boyle's expression remains fixed, but he gets the
message, or so Epstein assumes. Flannery believes that
he and Epstein are on equal footing, that he and the cops
are involved in an equitable exchange. He helps the cops.
The cops help him. This is decidedly not the case.

'So, Dave, what's the good news?' Epstein asks. He takes
a seat to Flannery's left, leaving Billy Boyle to sit down
across from the mobster. Though ostensibly one of Paulie
Margarine's subordinates, Dave 'Flabby Dave' Flannery
runs his own crew. Dave is twenty-eight and definitely on
the rise.

Flannery points to a pair of stuffed mushrooms on a plate
that once held a hot antipasto. 'Help yourself,' he advises.

'We ate.'

'You don't want nothin'?' Flannery's features are small
and squeezed together by his enormous cheeks. Looking at
the man, Epstein tries to decide whether his face is retreating
or advancing. Retreating, he finally decides. Eventually the

man's cheeks will meet and his face will look just like his ass.

'Espresso, for two,' Epstein says.

Flannery sucks down a glass of wine, then raises his arm to reveal the sapphire ring on his finger and the Rolex on his wrist. 'John,' he calls to the waiter, 'espresso for my friends. And you could bring the pasta.'

Epstein waits for Flannery to speak first, the wait stretching out until the waiter appears with a bowl of fettuccine Alfredo. He sets the bowl down and walks away. Flannery digs right in, expertly twirling the ribbons of pasta around his fork before jamming them into his mouth.

'Paulie's gonna go all out,' he says between bites.

'How so?'

'Don't know yet. But he wants to hit Toufiq hard. Ya know what I mean? Knock the little prick and his crew out of the game, for good and for ever.'

Epstein looks over at Billy Boyle, who's indeed beginning to boil. Flannery's attitude is dismissive, his tone weary, as if he owns the cops.

'But you're gonna call me, right?' Epstein asks. 'As soon as you know?'

The espresso arrives before Flannery can reply. Epstein waits for the waiter to fill the two small cups, then repeats the question. 'But you're gonna call me, right? Because my orders are real simple. Paulie Margarine starts a war, OCCB will arrest everybody in his organization. And that includes you, Dave. Plus, we'll hit every piece of your operation, including Ermine Escorts, which you only opened a month ago.'

Flannery eats in silence for several minutes, until the plate is empty. Then he signals to the waiter. 'You could bring the veal now.' Finally, he turns to Epstein. 'That's impressive. Ermine Escorts. How quick you connected me. But somethin's gotta give here. How do I know I won't get hit next?'

'How do you know Toufiq is responsible?' Epstein responds.

Flannery shakes his head. 'What you're sayin', it don't matter. Guys like us, we have to react. That's how we got be like us in the first place. Besides, with four guys down, I say we already got a war.'

Epstein reverts to his original point. 'We're not ready to move on Paulie,' he admits. 'We need another year. But we got enough to get indictments. Think of the cost, Dave. Think about lawyers who get four hundred dollars an hour. Think of the lost revenues. And all for nothing, because I've got snitches inside Toufiq's crew and they're tellin' the same story. Toufiq's not the source of your troubles.'

Another silence, a silence in which Epstein contemplates turning Flannery over to Billy Boyle. Epstein is still undecided when the veal shows up.

'Veal marsala,' Flannery says. 'They cook it right.'

Epstein finally nods to Billy Boyle, who reaches across the table to snatch Flannery's plate. When the plate's sitting in front of him, he spits into it. 'You don't call, ya fuckin' mutt,' he explains, 'I'll kill you myself.'

Their cards on the table, Epstein and Billy Boyle stand up to leave. But then Epstein has a change of heart and decides to throw Flannery a bone. Thinking, What the hell, he's not gonna eat the veal.

'Your boy, Carlo? You should warn him off that Ridgewood deal. It's gonna go bad.'

Eleven

Epstein lifts the sheet to look at what remains of Bruno Brunale's head. He's been warned, so he's not surprised by the gore. The man's head has been torn apart, exploded really, and strings of blood-saturated gray matter stream across the sidewalk. Worms deserting the skull, Epstein thinks before dropping the sheet.

According to Billy Boyle, who arrived first, the damage must have been done by a rifle loaded with hollow-point ammo, the kind used to bring down bear and buffalo. Meanwhile, nobody heard anything, nobody saw anything, which means the perp used a suppressor to control flash and noise. Suppressors are rare, effective suppressors anyway. But then, so are knives with Arabic inscriptions.

Bad news for Paulie Margarine, for the NYPD, too. A knife in Macy's, a rifle in Astoria. Another man, Charles Bousejian, was bludgeoned to death with an aluminum base-ball bat.

But there's good news here as well. A pair of uniformed cops on foot patrol responded to the Brunale shooting within a minute. What's more, they did their job, detaining all witnesses. That included Paulie Margarine, who was standing within a foot of Brunale when the fatal shot was fired. Epstein's been looking for an excuse to approach the gangster. Now he has it.

As Epstein turns away, his cell phone rings. He quickly retrieves it. Epstein's hoping to hear from Dave Flannery, but it's Champliss on the other end.

'What do you have for me?'

'I just got here, but I'm sure it's connected to the other homicides,' Epstein admits.

'And?'

'You're asking me what Paulie's gonna do next?'

'Yeah.'

'Paulie's gonna go after Toufiq. I have it from a reliable source.'

'And what are you gonna do?'

'I'm gonna talk him out of it.' Another of Epstein's little fibs. Postponement is the most he can deliver. 'I think he'll listen to reason.'

His superior mollified, Epstein takes a look around. The job's gone all out, shutting down Thirty-First Street for two blocks in either direction. People exiting the subway are being escorted to the nearest corner. Pedestrians hoping to enter are being told to hoof it to the next stop. Across the street, Epstein spots Paulie Margarine standing beside a uniformed officer assigned to make sure he doesn't leave. Epstein almost dances across the street, approaching to within a yard.

'You need to see a doctor?'

Paulie's blue coat is pockmarked with splatter. There are bits of skull and brain tissue in the man's hair. What hair he has left, anyway. To Epstein's mind, Paulie is aging badly. His face is deeply lined and he looks as though he hasn't slept in a week. The muscles of his shoulders and chest sag when he shifts his weight from one leg to the other.

But Paulie's attitude hasn't changed. 'Fuck you,' he says.

'Does that mean you're OK?' Epstein retrieves his ID and holds it up for Paulie's inspection. He notes a light of recognition blossom in Paulie's tired eyes when he reads OCCB. He's not dealing with a precinct dick.

'What do you say,' Epstein asks, 'we go take a seat and talk for a few minutes?'

The cell phone in Epstein's pocket begins to vibrate before Paulie responds. 'Think about it while I answer this,' Epstein says before moving off.

'Epstein here.'

'It's Flannery. I got what you asked for.'

'Shoot.'

'A birthday party at one of those restaurants where they smoke them pipes. I forget what they call 'em – hookers or somethin' like that. Paulie's gonna hit the joint hard. He's usin' out of state shooters. Swear to God, the old prick went on for an hour about the expense.'

'When, Dave? When is this supposed to happen?'

'He told me to make sure I had an alibi for eight o'clock tomorrow night.'

'And where's this going down?'

'Someplace near Steinway Street. I'm not sure exactly, but I can tell you the restaurant will be closed for a private party.'

Epstein remembers to thank his informant before hanging up, just as if Billy Boyle hadn't spit into Flannery's veal. 'You did good, Dave. I won't forget.'

Paulie Margarine shifts his weight from one leg to another when Epstein approaches him for the second time. Aware of Paulie's arthritis, Epstein assumes the man's knees are hurting.

'Well?' Epstein asks.

'Let's go,' Paulie says.

Epstein leads the gangster to an unmarked car three blocks away. Paulie shuffles along, his shoes scraping the sidewalk, but he doesn't complain. Epstein admires that.

In no hurry, Epstein unlocks the car, then opens a back door. He's curious now. Paulie knows that Epstein, should he be of mind, can lock him inside. Will he enter willingly? That would tell Epstein a good deal about the man's state of mind. But no, Paulie Margarine proves himself in control, despite his recent trauma.

'After you,' he says.

Epstein slides across the seat. He watches Paulie Margarine lower himself, one piece at a time, then work his legs into the car, watches the man lean back and sigh.

'So, whatta ya want?'

'You can tell me what happened, for starters.' Epstein's tone is mild. He's holding a wild card and he knows it.

'I was talkin' to Bruno and his head blew off. I didn't see nothin'. I'm bein' sincere. I didn't see a fuckin' thing and I didn't hear a fuckin' thing. One minute I'm talkin' to Bruno, the next I'm eatin' his brains.'

'Any idea where the shot came from?'

'A rooftop, a window, the el platform, a passing car? I got no idea.'

Epstein nods. 'But you'd have to agree, this guy's a real pro. I mean, he killed Tony Maguire in front of hundreds of witnesses and walked away. Brunale, he takes out with a sniper's rifle from god-knows-where. Yeah, that's right. What happened to Brunale wasn't caused by any handgun round. This is the kind of bullet that kills elephants.'

Paulie considers this for a moment, then says, 'So what?'

'So, do you really think that Rachid Toufiq, or any of this people, could do this?'

'I don't know what you're talkin' about.'

'That right?'

'That's exactly right.'

'Well, consider this. We know what you plan to do tomorrow night. You hear me? If any of your people stray to within a mile of that restaurant, we'll have your ass in jail before midnight.'

Paulie Margarine can't entirely control his surprise, though he makes a valiant effort by leaning forward to rub his knees.

'And what good would it do you, Paulie, even if Toufiq and his crew vanished from the face of the Earth? What would you buy except a little time? A very little.' Epstein shakes his head. 'You gotta start thinking outside the box, Paulie. There's has to be another way. One that works.'

Two hours later, from his desk at OCCB, Epstein watches a replay of Radisson's press conference, which took place in the late afternoon. To his surprise, Radisson doesn't flash his hole cards. He goes with the tape alone, running snippets, including the assault that killed Maguire. Held back are the knife and the non-secretor business, the perp surfacing at Columbus Circle and the preceding homicides, of Bousejian, Peterson and Terrentino. It's only after his opening statement, while he's taking questions, that a CBS reporter named Clarence Hartigan suggests a connection. Hartigan speaks precisely when Radisson acknowledges him. The room is crowded and he knows he won't get another chance.

'Charles Bousejian and Shawn Peterson, both homicide victims, and both with known ties to organized crime, were killed within hours of each other last Friday night. Is there any connection between their killings and the killing of Tony Maguire?'

When Radisson closes his eyes in relief, Epstein smiles. The reporter hasn't connected the victims to Paulie Margarine. Plus, he left out Nomo Terrentino. Radisson most likely feels good about his performance. The tape is raw meat and the public will eat it up.

'We're not discounting any possibility,' he tells Hartigan. 'Nothing's off the table.'

The reporters question Radisson for another fifteen minutes before the deputy chief calls a halt. By then, he's admitted that he has no reliable witnesses and no suspects. Not even a person of interest.

'We're counting on the public to come forward,' he explains, not for the first time. 'Somebody knows this man.'

Epstein shuts down his computer and gets to his feet. He needs to speak with a pair of detectives assigned to monitor a house in the Queens neighborhood of Ridgewood, another of his cases. And there's a note on his desk, from Sgt. Tina Metzenbaum, she of the Crime Scene Unit, about the possibility that the perp breathed hard enough on the display case to leave DNA evidence. By now, everybody working the case believes the perpetrator's had prior military experience. If so, his DNA will be on file.

An hour later, Epstein knocks on his boss's door. The last stop before he goes home to Sofia. Champliss is seated behind his desk, in shirtsleeves and suspenders. He sniffs as Epstein enters, lifting his nose.

'Good news?' he asks.

'CSU thinks the perp might have left DNA evidence when he breathed on the glass.'

'Might have?'

'We'll know in a day or two.'

'What about Marginella?'

Solly Epstein is big on wiggle room. Yeah, you can over-promise, at least most of the time, as long as you don't take it too far. But this isn't most of the time. He needs to deliver.

'For now, I bought twenty-four hours. But I think Paulie's a reasonable man. I'm trying to sell him on the fact that eliminating Toufiq won't solve his problems.'

'That's good, Solly. Do you think he's buying?'

'Actually, boss, I think if he decides not to attack Toufiq, it's because he's already decided to attack somebody else. Men like him, that's all they know.'

Twelve

Paulie Margarine isn't more than fifty feet from Epstein's unmarked car when the cell phone in his pocket, Thorpe's cell phone, trumpets the opening bars of the *William Tell Overture*.

Hi Yo fucking Silver. This is Paulie's first thought. Quickly followed by the fear that Thorpe is tracking his every movement, that Paulie's under surveillance right now, perhaps through the telescopic sight of the rifle that killed Bruno Brunale. But even that ugly possibility can't bring Paulie Margarine down. A path has opened before him, thanks to a dumb cop with a big mouth.

'Fuck you,' he says into the phone.

'No call for that. Business is business, after all.'

'You been watchin' too many *Godfather* movies.'

'Perhaps so. In any event, I thought it time we spoke again.'

'So speak, asshole.'

'My message remains simple. If you pay me off, I'll vanish. I bear you no animosity. I hold no grudge against you.'

Paulie shudders as a wave of hatred passes through his body. His eyes literally bulge in his head. But when he finally speaks, his voice is only slightly harsher than matter-of-fact.

'How much?'

'That's crude.'

'You havin' fun, Thorpe? You havin' a good time?'

'Three hundred and fifty thousand dollars.'

'And where am I supposed to get that kind of money?'

'From your account in Banco de Panama. I hear it runs to seven figures.'

Paulie's fingers tighten on the cell phone. Patience, he tells himself. Don't show this scumbag anything. 'Say, you know about cops and lying?'

'Illuminate me.'

Illuminate? Paulie imagines removing the flesh from Thorpe's bones with a potato peeler. But again, when he speaks, his voice is under control.

'The Supreme Court says cops can lie to suspects. Cops can say they found your fingerprints or DNA, or that you ran past a surveillance camera, even if you didn't. But suppose that you wore gloves that night, or you checked the block for cameras? In that case, you'd know the cops are lying because they haven't got any real evidence. Now you, Thorpe, you just showed me your hole card. My account doesn't run to anything like seven figures. If it did, I'd be livin' somewhere else besides Astoria, say on a yacht in the Bahamas.'

Thorpe takes a minute, then says, 'Well, as we're never to meet and have no way to settle the issue, we'll have to agree to disagree. The question's moot from my point of view anyway. This business I'm conducting, it's not without overhead. And there's also the element of time. Once the bargaining process begins, there's no end to the haggling.'

'So, it's three-fifty or nothin'?'

'I'm afraid so.'

'And how much time do I get?' Paulie is limping toward Ditmars Boulevard where he hopes to find a gypsy cab. His home is less than a mile away, but his knees are on fire. 'I'm not kiddin' about the account. There's nowhere near that kind of money in that account.'

'Are you're asking for good will? Are you agreeing to pay?'

'Do I have a fuckin' choice?' Paulie spots a cab on Thirty-First Street and waves to the driver. 'Look, I gotta go. I got business. Is there any way I can get in touch with you?'

'Afraid not.'

'Then call me tomorrow morning. I'll be home.'

Paulie's about to hang up, but Thorpe is too quick. 'I don't object to your tone, given the circumstances. In fact,

I admire your toughness, as I understand your need to regain equilibrium. Nevertheless, I sincerely advise you not to assume that you're somehow in control when you have no cards to play.'

Home again. Paulie makes two quick calls, the first to Ermine Escorts, the second to a hood named Oliver Havelock. At Ermine, he instructs Phyllis to put Lee Pho in a cab, pronto.

'And tell her to bring the Tiger Balm.'

'Your knees again?' Phyllis caps her question with a sympathetic cluck.

'They're killin' me,' Paulie admits.

Paulie's conversation with Oliver Havelock is even briefer. 'Get over here,' he commands before hanging up the phone.

Forty-five minutes later, when Lee Pho arrives first, Paulie is more annoyed than angry. Save for a single flaw, Oliver Havelock is everything Paulie could want in an underboss. He's loyal, tenacious, intelligent and utterly ruthless. But not once in his entire fucking life has he been on time.

Paulie escorts Lee Pho into the basement where he's set up a massage bench near the pool table. Lee Pho isn't the best looking whore in Dave Flannery's stable – her legs are too short and she's on the dumpy side – but Lee Pho has the hands of an angel. What's more, the woman speaks almost no English. Even in bed, Paulie has to use sign language to make his wants known.

The bell rings as Paulie strips down to his shorts, a pair of striped boxers. He hobbles back up the stairs and lets Havelock in.

'I got here as soon as I could.' Havelock is tall and lean, with a hatchet for a nose and eyes so close-set they're prac- tically touching. His nickname is Ollie Owl.

'Congratulations, you got beat by a whore,' Paulie observes.

'Say what?'

Paulie heads for the basement without explaining. Already stripped down to bra and panties, Lee Pho is arranging her creams and ointments next to the massage table. Paulie lies

down on his back. Lee Pho will do his knees first. He
doesn't have to tell her.

'She OK?' The Owl's lips come slightly apart as he
speaks, but his teeth remain together.

'Yeah, she don't understand English. But do me a favor,
turn on the stereo.' Paulie has the room swept for bugs twice
a month, but he's cautious anyway. For all he knows, the
FBI could be listening to him from a satellite. 'Just start
the CD player.'

A trumpet fanfare precedes Wilson Pickett's gravelly
voice. Pickett's doing *Stagger Lee*, loud enough to raise
Bruno Brunale from the dead. Havelock kneels at the head
of the massage table as Lee Pho applies a glob of tiger
balm to the side of Paulie's right knee. Though her touch
is gentle, Paulie winces. He winces again as her fingers
begin to probe, but then the ointment heats up and he starts
to relax. Paulie's not kidding himself. The only permanent
cures for what's ailing him are knee replacement or death,
and he's not sure which one he's looking forward to least.
But Lee Pho and her ointments will get him through what
promises to be a long night.

'The Flab took the bait,' Paulie tells Havelock.

'Yeah?'

'Yeah.'

In fact, there's no planned attack on Rachid Toufiq and
his little crew. There's only Paulie's near legendary ability
to sniff out rats and the obvious fact that Thorpe has to be
getting information from somebody. How else would he
know that Maguire, Bousejian and the rest were tied to
Paulie? Or that Paulie hangs out at Sweet's Bar? Or about
Paulie's bank account in Panama? That was a big mistake
Thorpe made, mentioning the name of the bank. Only a
few months before, Paulie had recommended Banco de
Panama to Flabby Flannery.

Paulie can recall the conversation almost word for word.
'These are bankers who know how to keep a fuckin' secret,'
he told the Flab. 'If you can manage the transportation
problem, you won't have to worry about the IRS freezing
your accounts.'

The Owl leans a bit closer. 'So, where do you wanna go with this?'

'First thing, find me an untraceable cell phone. Then reach out to that kid, the one who knows locks.'

'Clyde Redman?'

'Yeah, Clyde.' Paulie groans as Lee Pho begins to massage the sole of his left foot, her little fingers digging into the pressure points. He feels the tension leaking out. The anger, too. He has to get it right this time. The next few days will decide his future and his son's future. And it's not just the three-fifty. Paulie can manage the three-fifty. What worries Paulie is the next three-fifty and the one after that. Because that's exactly the way he'd play the game if he had some asshole where Thorpe has him. He'd suck the bastard dry.

'Are the Martinez brothers available?' he asks.

'I think Pedro's still in Rikers.'

'Then use John Gaglione's crew. We're lookin' for discreet here, right? No shots fired? Because I want that rat fuck alive, Ollie. Me and him, we gotta have a private talk.'

Thirteen

Paulie's parked on College Point Boulevard, only four blocks from the Flab's house, when he takes out his cell phone at midnight. He punches a number into the phone and the Owl picks up a minute later.

'You in place?' Paulie asks.

'We're in the back yard.'

'What's it look like?'

'One light, in a front room upstairs.'

'Good, good. I'll leave the line open. When he picks up, go in. And don't kill him.'

Paulie doesn't wait for an answer. He takes out a second phone, this one supplied by the Owl, and punches in Flannery's number.

'Dave, you still awake?' he asks when the Flab picks up. 'Because, me and you, we gotta talk.'

'What about?'

And that's another thing. Like Solly Epstein and Billy Boyle, Paulie Margarine doesn't care for the Flab's attitude. Flannery's a man without respect.

'About that thing tomorrow? I want you to take charge.'

'I thought you said you were usin' talent from out of state?'

'Dave, I need you to do this little thing for me. The outside talent, it fell through. A bad break, OK, but we gotta move on. Look, I'm comin' over. We'll talk it out.'

'Comin' over? Where are you now.'

'I'm only a few blocks from your house. Say, you still get that prosciutto from up on Arthur Avenue? Because I could definitely use a sandwich. I haven't eaten all night.'

The voice that responds is Oliver Havelock's, not Dave Flannery's. 'I'll see what's in the refrigerator.'

'He didn't give you any trouble?'

'Just handed me the phone, like he knew it was comin'. We do have a problem, though. He's got a woman here.'

'A girlfriend?'

'A pro.'

'Take the Flab into the basement and tie him down good. And tell Clyde to keep an eye on him. I'll be there in a minute.'

As it turns out, the prostitute is no problem whatever. Paulie takes her into a bedroom, shushing her as they go. He doesn't want to kill her, but he has no choice. Leave her alive and she'll shoot off her mouth to someone. Whores being whores. She pleads, of course, and cries. A not-so-young blonde with faint stretch marks on her belly.

'I have a daughter,' she tells him.

'I got a son,' Paulie replies. Then he nods to the Owl. 'No blood.'

Paulie heads for the basement, his intention to confront the Flab alone. The questions he needs to ask, about a man named Thorpe, are not for the ears of Ollie Havelock. Paulie's already told the Owl that Flannery is responsible for their troubles.

Paulie finds the Flab duct-taped to a chair in the basement. He's gagged, for good measure, and Clyde Redman's watching over him.

'Boss?'

Paulie nods to himself at Clyde's respectful tone. This is a good kid. 'The lock give you trouble?' he asks.

'Piece of cake.' Clyde Redman, who grew up in the Harlem but claims Apache heritage, is a lock and safe specialist. He's mostly used on heists, but his job tonight was unlocking the Flab's back door while Paulie kept him distracted.

'Go upstairs, tell the Owl I'll call him if I need him.'

Paulie waits until Clyde shuts the door leading into the kitchen, then explores the Flab's basement. As he goes, he snaps on a pair of latex gloves and dons a painter's mask. For once, he's not being paranoid. At a press conference just the other day, a spokeswoman for the Medical Examiner bragged that the ME's new lab can recover DNA from a fingerprint.

'I'm tryin' to get the picture, Dave,' Paulie says. 'Because I keep tellin' myself that I did right by you. I brought you into my thing, gave you work, treated you with respect. And what did you do by way of showin' me how grateful you were? You ratted me to the cops. Please, tell me what the fuck you were thinkin'. Did they have you in the hole? Were you facin' hard time? Or did you think you were gonna take my place? That a man like the Owl would kneel to kiss your ring?'

Paulie hefts a monkey wrench that has to be three feet long and weigh five pounds. He imagines himself crushing every bone in Flannery's body, starting with his toes. Paulie Margarine hates rats. But the wrench won't do, nor will an awl stuck in a joist or the hatchet he discovers on a workbench. No, you get blood on you, one fuckin' drop, you go away for the rest of your life.

Paulie finds what he's after on the floor next to the oil burner, a small propane torch. He twists the little wheel on the side before turning back to Flannery. The hiss of escaping gas seems to fill the room, to own the space. Paulie gives it a few seconds, then closes the valve. He turns to examine Flannery. The Flab has breasts like a woman, big hanging breasts, and the fat around his middle covers his cock and balls, a miniskirt of shapeless flesh. Paulie finds himself wondering what the whore felt when she first laid eyes on him. This was a body that couldn't be cleaned. But maybe she was used to it, maybe that was her specialty, repulsive men.

With a quick yank, Paulie rips the gag away. The Flab grimaces, but doesn't make a sound. His eyes are spitting hate.

'I was there when Bruno got whacked, which you already know,' he says. 'I was a witness. Swear to God, the cops wouldn't let me go until I talked to the detective. His name was Epstein, a name I'm sure you recognize.' Paulie slows down for a minute, but the Flab refuses to look at him. 'To make a long story short, this detective, Epstein, warned me off the hit on Toufiq. Only thing, Dave, there wasn't any hit on Toufiq. I made that up because I didn't trust you.'

Flannery finally looks up at his boss. 'You're gonna kill me.'

Though he doesn't hear a question, Paulie responds anyway. 'Don't be so pessimistic. You help me out, maybe we could work a deal.'

'What kind of deal?'

'I wanna hear about the set-up first, what you give, what you get, like that. We'll take it from there.'

The Flab's eyes roll across the room, to the left and the right, his neck twisting as far as it can, given the duct tape. Paulie wonders if he's looking for a way out, some magic eject button, or maybe for his guardian angel to ride to the rescue. But no, Paulie decides, the Flab's getting ready to lie. He's pickin' his words carefully.

'They had me for the Alterone thing,' Flannery says. 'They had me dead. I was lookin' at twenty-five to life.'

Paulie shrugs. He doesn't know the details and he doesn't want to. Carlo Alterone was a small-time coke dealer who set up on the Flab's turf without paying the required tax on his earnings. His body was found in a dumpster on Pitkin Avenue. End of story. Or, it would be if there was a word of truth to what the Flab was saying. But Paulie's not here for a debate. The cop is the least of his worries.

'Now tell me about Thorpe,' he says.

'Thorpe?'

'Yeah, tell me about Thorpe.'

'Thorpe?'

'Don't keep sayin' his name, Dave. You're getting' me crazy. Just tell me how you met him, how you met Thorpe. Let's start with that.'

Flannery's face tightens down when Paulie lights the propane torch. 'Swear to God, Paulie, swear on my fuckin' mother, I don't know what you're talkin' about.'

Paulie's never heard such despair in the voice of another

human being. For just a moment, he feels that despair himself. Flannery's telling the truth, which leaves Paulie Margarine with no bargaining power, no juice, no edge. Nevertheless, because he needs to be certain, Paulie sets down the torch and re-tapes the Flab's mouth.

'I'm gonna start with your hand, Dave, your right hand. Then I'm gonna ask you again. I'm gonna ask you to tell me how you met Thorpe. And don't even think about lyin' to me, because I can keep burning a lot longer than you can keep lying. You can trust me on that.'

As Paulie approaches the Flab, he experiences a moment, a transient moment, of sympathy. Not for the Flab, or the whore upstairs, who's most likely dead already. But for Ollie Havelock, the Owl. Dave Flannery must weigh 350 pounds. Disposing of his body will be no walk in the park. If the Owl didn't cart Flannery off in pieces, he was gonna need a crane to get him out of the basement.

Fourteen

Carter intends to make short work of Titanic Metal Fencing. A meatball, that's how he defines the task before him. To Carter's immediate superior in Afghanistan, Lieutenant Petronello, every assignment was a meatball, no matter how dangerous. But Titanic Metal Fencing really is a meatball. First thing, its yard, which takes up a short, triangular block, is marked by haphazardly arranged stacks of fencing material, from chain link to chicken wire, some reaching to a height of twenty feet. At this time of night, with the moon already down, their shadows dominate the yard. Carter's instinctively fond of shadows, and he's been trained to use them to his advantage.

But there's still the dog, some kind of terrier with filthy brown fur and a cropped tail, barking at Carter from behind a fence topped with strands of rusty barbed wire. The animal has to be neutralized, obviously, but Carter has a thing about collateral damage, a line he drew for himself years before. Men like Tony Maguire and Charles Bousejian? They'd chosen their lives freely and Carter had eliminated them without a second thought, as he'd eliminated Arab fighters in the Afghani mountains. But not the innocent, the villagers huddled in their stone huts, and not the miners in Sierra Leone, the ones who pulled diamonds from the riverbeds and went to sleep hungry at night. Not them.

Carter's love of precision contributes to his attitude. If you don't separate combatants from civilians, chaos will surely follow. Carter fears chaos. At times, especially in Africa, he stood inches from the edge of that abyss before stepping back. He didn't want the blood to own him as it owned so many of the others. Survival? Kill or be killed?

That was all fine. As was looting the looters. But not anyone anywhere, just because they happened to get in the way.

The mutt has stopped barking. He's now staring at Carter with his head cocked to the right, growling low in his chest. Carter is kneeling by the fence, unmoving. He thinks the animal is wondering why this human doesn't run away, or throw a rock, or do something besides stare back. The night is very cold and the dog's wet breath seems to explode from his mouth.

Carter removes a pair of bolt cutters from his backpack and cuts a small hole in the fence. He stretches the hole with both hands, then pulls the opening toward him before thrusting his right hand into the yard beyond. This is too much for the dog, who roars once, then leaps forward, throwing caution to the wind. Carter smiles as he yanks his fingers back through the opening. As anticipated, the animal's snarling muzzle follows, then his head, then his neck. By the time Carter's hands encircle the dog's mouth, he's thoroughly helpless.

Carter tightens down hard, then harder, until the dog squeals like a hurt puppy. Though Carter's repulsed by the greasy fur and the animal's sour smell, he holds on for a moment longer, his aim to drive home an underlying basic. He's in a hurry and there won't be time for another lesson.

The dog yanks himself free of the fence, his legs skidding on the concrete, when Carter lets go of his muzzle. Then he hurtles across the yard and dives under a truck parked near the gate, still howling and without looking back.

'Good dog,' Carter says.

Once through the fence, Carter approaches the back of a single-story building on the northwest corner of the site. The building's few windows are protected by iron bars that project far enough to cage an air conditioner. Carter uses one of these cages as a stepping stone to the flat roof, a nothing climb. Working quickly now, he cuts a hole in the roof with a hatchet, then slides down a rope to the floor twenty feet below.

The only light, from a street lamp at the end of the block, barely penetrates the filthy windows at the front of the building. It takes nearly a minute before Carter's pupils fully adjust to the darkness. Then he instinctively makes his way toward the light, coming around a stack of cast-iron bars to discover a Ford Econoline parked just behind a roll-up door. Good enough.

Carter slips off his backpack and lays it on the floor. He removes a small bar of Semtex, a detonator and a timer. Connecting them, one to the other, takes only a few seconds, setting the timer for thirty minutes only a few seconds more. Finally he attaches the bomb to the Econoline's gas tank and starts the timer.

A meatball. And he didn't have to kill the mutt, either.

Carter walks into his apartment thirty-five minutes later. He heads for the kitchen where he makes himself a sandwich, ham and Swiss on seven-grain bread. He fills a glass with milk, adding a dollop of chocolate syrup at the last minute. The curious thing about Carter is that he has no real use for the money he accumulates. He has no wish to dine in Manhattan's four-star restaurants, or to cruise the Avenues in a stretch Hummer. Carter accumulates only to accumulate. The numbers that matter are the ones on his bank statements, and it doesn't bother him at all if no one else ever sees them. Carter doesn't crave admiration, much less celebrity.

He eats standing up, chewing thoughtfully. A few ounces of Semtex aren't enough to make anyone scream terrorist and it's possible the explosive will go entirely undetected. But there was definitely enough to blow the Econoline's gas tank and start a serious fire. Maybe the fencing material, the metal, will survive. But the office, just a few yards away, is certain to be destroyed. Paulie Margarine has an interest in Empire Fencing. Hopefully, he and his legit partner are insured. That way, should the insurance company pay up, they'll have a chance to rebuild the company. Like Thorpe, Carter bears no grudge against Paulie.

Carter washes the dishes before retreating to his computer. He opens Outlook Express, then considers for a moment before typing an e-mail addressed to Thorpe. Though he's really fed up, he opts for a neutral tone. *Bravo is complete.*

Please forward all past due remittances. He wants to add,
If the operation is to proceed. But he merely signs his name
and sends it off. That done, he turns to a computer game,
The Battle of Bull Run. Carter has chosen the part of the
Union Army, playing against the computer. His job is to
reverse history, the Union army having been soundly
defeated at Bull Run. Though Carter's not usually a gambler,
he's decided to risk everything on a frontal assault. He will
feint to the left and right, then slam his main force into the
heart of Beauregard's line. But that comes later. For now,
he must decide where to deploy his troops. Though the men
need rest after a two-day forced march, an attack must be
launched before Confederate reinforcements arrive. Delay
was McDowell's first mistake.

Carter's still at it a half-hour later when Thorpe replies
to his e-mail. The message is short, but Carter reads the
words several times. He wants to make sure he gets the
facts right. Thorpe is claiming that their 'partnership' will
soon 'bear fruit', that Paulie Margarine's resistance 'crum-
bles as we speak'. This is a sop to blunt the bad news.
*Problems with cash flow, as discussed in the past, preclude
immediate payment. Sorry, old boy. Keep the faith.*

Old boy? Faith? Carter has to wonder if Thorpe means
to piss him off. He has to wonder, too, about the magic
number. That's the number beyond which the benefits of
not paying Carter exceed the risks. Thorpe owes him twenty
for Maguire, twenty for Brunale, and eight for the arson.
$48,000? The brutal fact is that Carter's replaceable. There
are thousands more out there like him, maybe tens of thousands, from Rumania and Hungary and Russia, Cold War
veterans with hearts of stone, and from the crucible of
western Africa and the paramilitary armies of Columbia
and Peru. Not all are as skilled as Carter, and not all share
his self-control, much less his ability to blend in. But
Thorpe's tapped into a network that includes hundreds of
mercenaries. If he decides to make a switch, personnel will
be the least of his problems.

Carter shuts down the computer and prepares for bed.
He's brushing his teeth, staring into the mirror at his foaming

mouth, when he makes a pair of admissions. First, Thorpe isn't lying; they did talk about future cash-flow problems before they shook hands in Dar es Salaam. Thorpe had been straightforward. His funds were limited and there might come a time, especially in the course of this first operation, when Carter would have to wait for his money.

All very nice, every track covered. But Thorpe has a gift for intrigue that Carter will never match. Carter knows this, as he knows it's entirely possible, perhaps likely, that Thorpe anticipated this moment. That he foresaw a scenario in which the mark was about to make good, while Carter was still owed a ton of money. Maybe dumping Carter was always a part of Thorpe's business plan.

Carter imagines receiving a pink slip in the mail, imagines being fired, and laughs. His notice of termination will be delivered in the form of a bullet. Without doubt.

Well, live by the gun, die by the gun, an equation that works equally well no matter who's on the dying end.

For Carter, sleep is a skill, one he picked up in Afghanistan when every cell in his body demanded vigilance. You had to sleep, you had to eat, you had to clean your weapon, you had to have ammo, you had to exploit your technological advantages. As far as Carter's concerned, there's no essential difference between any of these imperatives. Thus he sleeps soundly for the next four hours and wakes up refreshed. With nothing to do. With no further assignment.

Good news, maybe. At least Thorpe's debt to him isn't growing.

By four o'clock that afternoon, Carter has moved out of his Astoria apartment and into Janie's Woodside co-op. He takes only his personal possessions, leaving the furniture and the kitchenware behind. The move attracts attention from three of Janie's neighbors. This is unavoidable and Carter patiently explains that he's Janie's brother. One, a young woman, asks about Janie's condition.

'She was always so brave,' the woman tells Carter. 'She was like a role model for me.'

'I visit her every day and I can tell you that she's still

brave,' Carter declares. 'But I don't think she'll be coming home again.'

'That's a shame. I'm so sorry.'

The good news is that he'll be accepted once the word gets around. The bad news is that he'll be remembered. But there's no alternative, not in the short run. The thing about Thorpe is that he likes to talk, but hates to listen. Never, in the time they spent together, did he inquire into Carter's personal life. Thorpe knows nothing of Janie, much less her cozy apartment. Now it's a question of who will be the first to break cover.

But maybe it won't come to that. Maybe the mark is ready to fork out and maybe Thorpe will pay up, maybe they'll both move on to some new challenge.

Hope for the best, plan for the worst.

Carter walks into the Cabrini Nursing Center at six o'clock. Dinner is being served and most of the staff and the patients are gathered in the dining room. But not Janie. Janie's food travels from a plastic bag down through a rubber tube that passes through her abdomen and into her stomach.

Though Janie's sleeping when Carter enters, a television on the far side of her bed is tuned to CNN. Wolf Blitzer and a pair of experts are commenting on the video taken by the surveillance cameras in Macy's.

'Let's roll the tape,' Blitzer says.

Fascinated, Carter watches himself commit a murder. He feels a certain amount of pride – at no point does he reveal his face, and his movements are extremely precise, from the withdrawal of the knife to its final placement. But maybe he shouldn't congratulate himself too quickly. The truth is that he hadn't felt anything approaching an emotion when he killed Tony Maguire. His focus was entirely on the job, as though he was a trapeze artist performing an especially difficult trick. Or, better yet, a machine programmed to accomplish a specific end, a machine whose programming didn't include second thoughts.

This wasn't always the case. The first time Carter executed another man, he and Cornelius Halbert were operating as a sniper unit in the hills of Tora Bora. A veteran of Gulf One, Halbert was the spotter, Carter the marksman.

'Target at two o'clock, back there in the shadows across the gorge.' A black man from rural South Carolina, Halbert spoke slowly and with a pronounced drawl.

'Got him.'

Peering through the 10X scope, Carter instantly recognized another human being. An enemy, true, weapon in hand, wearing the black-and-white keffiyeh of a Palestinian fighter. But still a human being.

'You waitin' for exactly what?' Halbert whispered into his ear. 'You hopin' he'll have a heart attack, maybe die of a stroke?'

As he pulled the trigger, Carter sensed that he was crossing into another world, a parallel world with its own customs. A year later, a Nepalese mercenary who called himself Lo Phet gave this world a name.

'We already die, go to hell world,' Lo Phet explained over a bottle of Australian wine in Kirkuk.

'Hell world?'

Phet's smile exposed a set of worn brown teeth. He used those teeth to rip off a chunk of tobacco from a slimy plug he carried in his shirt pocket. 'Hell world better,' he said.

'Better than what?'

'Better than world of hungry ghosts.'

Though Carter failed to get the joke, Lo Phet chortled for the next ten minutes. By then, Carter was killing without a second thought.

Janie's eyes are open when Carter turns away from the TV. She blinks twice, then twice again. This means that she wants to spell out a message. Carter has no objection, but the process is necessarily slow and he shortens it by dividing the alphabet in half, *A* to *K*, or *L* to *Z*.

'*A* to *K*?' Carter asks.

Blink.

Carter begins to recite the alphabet, stopping at *B* when Janie blinks. Again he asks, '*A* to *K*?' Again Janie blinks. This time Carter get to *I* before Janie stops him.

'Bible?' he guesses.

Blink.

'You want me to read?'

Janie blinks twice and Carter continues to work the alphabet until his sister's message is clear: 'Bible, do you feel it?'

Carter wants to ask, Feel what? but he doesn't have the nerve. From early on, Janie had demonstrated a talent for reaching into his mind. He couldn't lie to her, and he eventually stopped trying.

'The words are for you, not me,' he says. 'The words don't apply to me.'

What can you see in a paralyzed face? The mouth, the chin, the flesh covering Janie's cheekbones and along her jaw, all remain slack. There's no shake of the head, no disapproving frown, no stern lecture. But Carter reads the bottom line. He realizes that his sister hasn't bought any of his lies. Salesman for a French sporting goods manufacturer? Yeah, right.

'Should I read?' he asks.

Blink.

'Be diligent to know the countenance of thy cattle, and consider thy own flocks. For thou shalt not always have power, but a crown shall be given to generation and generation. The meadows are open, and the green herbs have appeared, and the hay is gathered out of the mountains. Lambs are for thy clothing, and the goats are the price of the field. Let the milk of the goats be enough for thy food, and for the necessities of thy house.'

An hour later, as Carter's about to leave, he leans forward to kiss his sister's forehead. 'I love you, big sister,' he says.

Carter settles down in Janie's apartment at eight o'clock that night. The apartment is fully furnished, perhaps over-furnished. The living room is crammed with upholstered chairs, polished tables and bookcases filled to overflowing. A long couch nearly covers a side wall. The bedroom contains an armoire, a triple dresser and a king-sized bed. It smells faintly of the powders and perfumes arranged on a vanity table next to an open bible. In the small kitchen, the counters are crammed with gadgets, a Cuisinart, a blender, a crock pot, a deep fryer, an electric can opener. A linen closet in the hall encloses enough sheets, blankets and towels to outfit a platoon.

There's a reasonable chance that Carter will eventually inherit the apartment, along with Janie's modest savings, and he tries to imagine himself settled down, maybe after he kills Thorpe. But that can never happen. Carter's spent the better part of his adult life prepared to move on a minute's notice. His profession – freely chosen, he reminds himself – demands mobility. At any moment, he might be forced to retreat, to place himself beyond the reach of an adversary. That's why he has a half-dozen passports from a half-dozen nations tucked into a half-dozen safe deposit boxes.

Ten minutes later, his future decided, Carter settles down before his computer. He checks his e-mail, but the only message is from a spammer who wants to sell him a septic system. Carter's been hoping against hope that his pal, Thorpe, would finally come across. But Thorpe hasn't even bothered to respond. Well, Carter tells himself, at least he got one thing right. Maybe he'll never settle into the sort of life most people take for granted, but he's definitely going to kill Montgomery Thorpe at the earliest opportunity. Either that, or be killed himself.

Fifteen

Epstein has come to hate Dr Gwen Morgan's office. Morgan is Sofia's obstetrician and her office is straight-ahead cutesy. There's a pink wall and a blue wall, and lots of lambs and puppy dogs and babies frolicking in kelly-green meadows. Yellow, black, red and white, the rug rats are as healthy as cherubs, while the skies above are as inno-cent as the kids themselves. Like any cop, Solly Epstein knows that life is a moment-to-moment crapshoot, and the atmosphere is an affront to his sensibilities. But the murals aren't the worst, not by a long shot. No, the worst is the total disconnection between the serendipity of the décor and the way Dr Morgan treats her patients. As on every other visit, all the chairs are taken when Epstein enters the office, Sofia clinging to his arm. This means that Sofia will have to wait a good ninety minutes before being ushered into an examining room, told to strip, then left to wait some more.

Without hesitation, a man gets up to offer Sofia his seat, leaving Epstein to stand, his arms crossed as he tries to contain his anger. From early on, he urged his wife to change obstetricians. His argument was simple: if your doctor treats you this badly in a public setting, what will she do in the privacy of the delivery room? Say, if you're unconscious?

But Sofia would not be moved. She offered the packed waiting room as evidence of Morgan's skills. If all these people were willing to put up with a ninety-minute wait, how bad could she be? Plus, there weren't many obstetri-cians out there, what with the lawyers ready to pounce if the kid was born cross-eyed.

Epstein looks down at Sofia, at her broad forehead and sharp nose. He's thinking that maybe she's experiencing a moment of regret, what with her back aching 24/7 and having to pee every ten minutes. Sofia has her arms wrapped around her belly and she's staring at a clock in the shape of a kitten. The clock is mounted on the far wall behind a counter that shields the clerical staff. There are three of them today, in pink scrubs, and they work non-stop, pulling charts, verifying insurance referrals and making appointments. Epstein wonders if they feel the hot waves of animosity that roll toward them, as he did when he was on foot patrol in the South Bronx. If looks were bullets, Sofia would already be collecting his death benefits.

An hour later, as the room gradually clears out, Epstein finds a seat next to his wife. By now, Sofia's been to the ladies' room three times, as have two other late-term women. A fourth woman, her stomach flat as a board, has also been running back and forth, in her case to throw up. And that's another thing. Only one bathroom? You'd think, given her specialty, that Morgan would have made allowances. A few square feet of productive space surrendered to her patients' comfort? Was that too much to ask? Especially with the endless waits?

'How ya doin'?' he says to his wife for the fifth time.

Sofia takes his hand. 'I spoke to my sister this morning before we came over. She's up against it, Solly.'

Epstein's grin is admiring. As always, Sofia's timing is flawless. His wife's sister, Eleana, is asking for a loan because her investment-counselor husband is under a RICO indictment for his role in a pyramid scheme. This is the same husband who once lived in a Manhattan penthouse and drove a vintage Mercedes, who lorded it over Epstein at family gatherings. The same husband who is now unable to pay his lawyers or feed his family.

'We've been through this.' Epstein struggles to keep his tone neutral. He's in a waiting room, surrounded by strangers, which is why Sofia chose this moment to bring up the subject. Epstein doesn't object to helping Sofia's sister and her two children. In fact, he's eager to help. It's just that he knows Alex will funnel the money to his lawyers and Eleana will have her hand out again within a week.

Epstein gives Sofia's arm an affectionate squeeze. 'Look, it's your money as much as mine. But think about what happened last time.'

'I know, Solly, but she's my sister. Her kid's are my nephews. *La familia*? I can't just throw that over.'

Sofia lapses into a momentary silence, her eyes returning to the clock on the far wall, then changes the subject. 'When I read that book about the joys of motherhood, nobody mentioned this part.'

Epstein looks at the clerks. He wants them to suffer as his wife is suffering, as every woman in the room suffers, a matter of fairness. He wants Dr Morgan to suffer, too, but she remains out of sight.

'We should've dumped this asshole a long time ago,' he says.

Epstein's voice is loud enough to attract the attention of the woman sitting next to Sofia. 'You'd be wasting your time,' she declares. 'I've been to three and it's always the same deal. Your time is their time.'

The phone clipped to Epstein's belt starts to vibrate before he can respond. He answers to find a detective named Lemlem Takile on the other end. The son of Ethiopian immigrants, Takile's nickname is Flash. Not because he's quick, though he is. Lemlem has the darkest skin and whitest teeth that Epstein's ever seen. His smile is a strobe light in a dark alley.

'I gotta take this outside,' Epstein tells Sofia before retreating to the hallway. When the door closes behind him, he says, 'Let's hear that again.'

Epstein listens for a minute, then says, 'Don't move until I get there. And I don't know exactly when that'll be. I'm at the doctor's with my wife. But what I'll do is call Billy Boyle, tell him to keep you company.' After a pause, he adds, 'You did good, Flash.'

Epstein pulls up in front of the Orchid Hotel some three hours later. He backs into a space marked 'Loading Zone – No Standing' and shuts off the engine. A liveried doorman rushes up to open the door, but stops abruptly when Epstein displays his lieutenant's shield. Epstein opens his own door and gets out.

'The security office,' he announces, 'Marty Benderman.'

Only steps from Central Park and Lincoln Center, the Orchid Hotel is an odd duck in this part of Manhattan, a decidedly second-rate establishment in an environment dominated by four-star behemoths. The doorman's old enough to be Epstein's father. His sky-blue uniform is shiny with age and his gold-piped trousers sag at the knees. Epstein thinks that maybe it's some kind of hotel karma. The Orchid harkens back to the bad old days when this stretch of Broadway was called Needle Park.

'Through the lobby, to the right, past the elevators.'

Epstein's about to brush by, when the doorman stops him. His smile reveals missing teeth on both sides of his mouth. 'This ain't about me, is it?'

At another time, Epstein would be tempted to play with the man's head, maybe ask, 'I don't know, what'd you do?' But he's already three hours late and he walks past the man without speaking.

The Orchid's security office is surprisingly modern and far better organized than OCCB's media room. Three tiers of small monitors reach into the hotel's every public space, the lobby, hallways, bar and restaurant, even the roof. A uniformed security guard sits in front of the monitors. His chair is wheeled and he slides back and forth, maybe trying to impress Billy Boyle and the Flash, who stand behind him.

'Boss, I think we got the asshole.' Lemlem Takile hits Epstein with his thousand-watter, a smile so disarming that Epstein instinctively returns it, all memory of the nightmare traffic between his Bay Ridge home and mid-town Manhattan suddenly erased.

'I heard that one already,' Epstein says. He wants to add something more, but Billy Boyle's dark blue eyes stop him cold. 'Where's this guy Benderman?'

Marty Benderman's office is nicely turned-out. There's lots of dark paneling, a decent rug, even a model sail-boat on a low bookcase. But the man himself is a wreck.

Thin as a rail, his hollow cheeks are some unnamed color between yellow and green. When he speaks, he holds a plastic tube to a hole in his throat and his voice sounds even worse than the computer-generated voice on the NYPD's automated phone menu.

'I can't give you the tape. Sorry. You'll have to get a subpoena.'

Billy Boyle is quick to explain. 'The hotel's owned by a multinational operating out of Zurich. From what Marty tells me, it takes three months to get permission to buy a broom.'

'Four,' Benderman croaks.

Epstein shrugs. 'What do you say we take a look?'

Shot forty minutes after Tony Maguire's death, the tape reveals a bearded man wearing a wide-brimmed fedora walking through the lobby and into the men's room. The fedora is gone when he emerges a short time later, likewise the beard, and there's a package tucked beneath his right arm. Instinctively, Epstein brings his eyes closer to the monitor on Benderman's desk.

The perp is walking with his head down and seems to be using the hotel's patrons to shield himself, but for one brief moment, as he emerges from behind a column, he's in full view of the camera. Predictably, the tape is grainy, with the man's over-exposed face an almost featureless blur. A male Caucasian, late twenties to early thirties, wearing a light-colored jacket without a visible logo. He might be anybody.

The man exits the hotel a few seconds later, but Epstein remains focused on the screen for another moment. Then he steps back. Twenty-four hours to secure and serve the subpoena, another day for the crime lab to enhance the image. Champliss and Radisson will be overjoyed.

'You speak to the doorman?' he asks Takile.

'Yeah, he doesn't remember the guy. Too long ago, too many people coming and going.'

Epstein nods, then heads for the hotel's lobby where he phones his contact at the Crime Scene Unit, Tina Metzenbaum. He gets her at home, a one-bedroom apartment in Jackson Heights. 'Hey, lover,' he says. 'Did I catch you at a bad time?'

In fact, Epstein and Tina aren't lovers and never have been. But they like to flirt and Tina says, 'Actually, my girlfriend just left.'

'Girlfriend?'

'The one with the tattoos. You wanna spring for the tape?'

'You toss in the video with the dwarf and I'll sign over my pension.'

Tina laughs on cue, then says, 'So, what's up, Solly?'

'The DNA thing you mentioned the other day. How did that turn out?'

'Nix on human DNA. Not enough material. But we'll get mitochondrial DNA for sure.'

Epstein knows two things about mitochondria. They live inside human cells and they have their own DNA. But the rest of it, especially the use of mitochondrial DNA as evidence, is hazy to him.

'Refresh me,' he says.

'Human DNA is a mix of genes inherited from both parents, but mitochondria come entirely from the mother. You understand? Every individual in the female line inherits mitochondria with the same DNA.'

'That could be a lot of people.'

'Bothers and sisters, first and second cousins, aunts and uncles. But if you can eliminate family members, the odds against any two unrelated individuals sharing the same mitochondrial DNA are roughly five thousand to one.'

Sixteen

Epstein's thinking, more and more, that Tony Maguire's killer will soon be identified. This is a big change and requires a serious adjustment to his strategy. His strategy for personal survival. But at the same time, Epstein's judgment is clouded by a swelling resentment. The incident in Macy's should never have happened. Showboating was what it was, a bush league play that elevated the perp from a bit player to public enemy number one. And what was the point? There was no rush. Maguire might have been eliminated a day or two later without any loss to the overall operation.

War is deception? Fine, but so is flying under the NYPD's (not to mention the New York media's) radar screen.

Ever dutiful nevertheless, Epstein reports the mitochondrial DNA evidence and the new video to Champliss within minutes of returning to headquarters. 'Right now, the video's too grainy for an ID, but I'm hoping the lab rats can spruce it up. Either way, you can take it to the public.'

Champliss sniffs. To indicate disdain? Apparently not, because he says, 'You bust this asshole, nobody's going to forget. I promise you that. Christmas? Macy's? The perp might as well have spit in the commissioner's face.'

Duty done and congratulations accepted, Epstein returns to Marty Benderman's office. He thanks Benderman, assuring him that a subpoena will be served tomorrow morning. Benderman nods once, then goes into his desk drawer for a long fat cigar. Epstein watches in disbelief, thinking that Benderman's about to jam the cigar into the hole in his throat. But the Hotel Orchid's security chief merely runs the cigar under his nose.

'I was on the job for twenty years,' he declares. 'If it was up to me, you'd walk out of here with the tape in your pocket.'

Epstein brings his partner home for dinner. He makes a phone call on the way, to Sofia, asking which she'd prefer, Chinese, Japanese, Italian or Indian. He's hoping she won't ask for mandongo soup, a Puerto Rican specialty that contains tripe and brains among its many dubious ingredients, and he's pleased when she announces a craving for lamb dupiaz and a roti stuffed with spiced potatoes. Sofia isn't all that happy when Billy Boyle walks through the door, nor when Epstein tells her that his day is far from done. He'll be leaving again right after dinner and won't be home until late.

'We're this close.' He spreads his fingers an inch apart. 'I'm hoping to wrap the case up before you go into labor. You know, feather in the cap, credit where credit is due.' He goes on to tell Sofia about the new video tape, finally adding, 'Checking surveillance cameras around Columbus Circle was my idea.'

Billy Boyle observes this bit of braggadocio without changing expression. A veteran of the first Iraq war, he made the singular mistake of volunteering for the reserves after his discharge from the Marine Corps. He didn't complain when he was called to active duty in Iraq II, but he came home more taciturn than ever.

After dinner and coffee – Bustelo, hot and super-strong – Epstein and Billy Boyle head for Astoria, with Billy driving. This is the second time Epstein has crossed Brooklyn and the traffic isn't any lighter. From the Belt to the Gowanus to the BQE and over the Kosciusko Bridge, they have to fight for every mile. Christmas shoppers, most likely, but Epstein's thoughts are anything but charitable. And given this particular errand, maybe that's for the best.

Billy Boyle's edging Epstein's Toyota past an accident when Epstein tries to call Dave Flannery. The Flab doesn't answer and Epstein hangs up without leaving a message. There's a distinct possibility that Flannery's dead, but

Epstein isn't overly concerned. Flannery was a marked man before Epstein spoke to Paulie Margarine. All the nonsense about a massacre at Toufiq's birthday party was a set-up, pure and simple. According to Epstein's long-time snitch, Fouad Birou, as well as the newly-acquired Ibrahim El-Shaer, not only is Toufiq's birthday in August, he isn't in New York. Epstein didn't know that when he confronted Paulie Margarine, but still . . .

Epstein glances at his watch as Billy Boyle eases the Toyota into a parking space before a non-descript apartment house on Newton Avenue. Eight stories of grimy yellow brick, the building occupies most of the block. Epstein knows, even before the super let's them in, that he'll find two elevators, one on either side of the building, and two stairways. He leads Billy Boyle up one of these stairways, to the third floor and apartment 3G. A hand-written sign greets them: *Jerry, I'm in the basement, in the laundry room. Come down and I'll give you the key. Carter.*

Billy Boyle grunts. Pleased to know that Carter resides at this address? Or annoyed because the man isn't home? Epstein isn't sure. He looks down at the far end of the hall where three kids play with a toy fire truck. Their laughter echoes in the confined space and Carter watches them for a moment, thinking that this is their time, three days before Christmas. They seem barely able to contain themselves, which is most likely why they were encouraged to play in the hall.

'What I'll do is go down to the basement, see if he's there,' Epstein says.

'We should both go,' Boyle responds. 'We're not talkin' about some pussy here.' For Billy Boyle, this is almost a speech.

'There are two elevators and two sets of stairs. Suppose we pass him? Suppose one of those kids tells him that two strangers were knockin' on his door? We lose the element of surprise, we got nothin'.'

'Then let me go.'

Epstein shakes his head. He's hoping to keep the initial contact low-key. 'Wait here. If I need you, I'll speed-dial your cell. You hear it ring and there's nobody on the other end, come running.'

Billy Boyle's grunt is lost on Epstein, who heads for the stairs, the elevator being too noisy. He descends slowly, flight by flight, until he finds himself in a huge storage area. Furniture, trunks, suitcases, rugs, bicycles and small appliances heaped to shoulder height in no apparent order. A narrow aisle leads past this chaos to an open doorway at the other end of the building. From where he stands, Epstein can see a pair of washing machines, one of them vibrating rapidly. But there's no one in view.

Despite his low-key intentions, Epstein brings his hand to the weapon beneath his unbuttoned coat and starts off down the aisle, his eyes moving from the laundry room ahead to the junk on his right. Except for the odd cockroach, his search uncovers no threat, and he's close to relaxed as he passes the halfway point. But then the lights go out and the basement is plunged into a darkness as profound as the one that greeted Jonah in the belly of the beast. The fear that seizes Epstein by the throat is equally profound. He reaches out to touch the wall on his left and takes a step before remembering to draw his weapon. Ahead, the washing machine suddenly begins to fill and the sound of the water flowing into the tub is loud enough to be an onrushing flood.

Time becomes physical for Epstein, the seconds weighed down by gravity. He doesn't see his life pass before his eyes, not yet. But when he feels the point of Carter's knife against his throat and Carter's hand settles over his own hand, the one holding his weapon, Epstein is unable to suppress a tiny moan. He gives up his gun without a fight and submits to a pat down that uncovers his badge. At no point does the knife at his throat even waver.

'How do you know Thorpe?'

Epstein's left hand is already in his coat pocket, cupped around his cell phone. All he need do is press the little button and Billy Boyle will ride to the rescue. But Epstein's afraid. He hears Sofia's voice, as clearly as if she were present. '*La familia*. I can't just throw that off.'

No, you can't, he thinks. You have to at least make an effort. 'My partner was in Iraq. That's where he met Thorpe.'

'What did he do in Iraq?'

'I don't know. He doesn't talk about it.'

'Where is he now?'

'Standing in front of your door.'

'That doesn't give us much time.'

Epstein wants to take a deep breath, but he knows that would be a tell. He has to remain calm, matter-of-fact, though he feels as if his bladder is about to explode. The man holding a knife to his throat has executed five men. At the very least.

'You wouldn't consider taking that knife away from my throat?' he asks.

'No, I wouldn't.'

'For Christ's sake, man, we came to give you a heads-up. We have video tape of you leaving the Orchid Hotel. Plus, you left mitochondrial DNA on a display counter in Macy's. You have to move on.'

'What do you do for Thorpe?'

The question surprises Epstein. 'I'm assigned to OCCB.'

'OCCB?'

'The Organized Crime Control Bureau. In the NYPD. I have access to their files.' Epstein pauses, hoping for a reply that doesn't come. 'I feed Thorpe information. He calls me his intelligence officer.'

Carter's soft laughter is obscene. 'If Thorpe wanted to warn me, he could have done it himself with a few key strokes. You came here to execute me. Do you deny that?'

When Epstein fails to answer, the tip of the knife cuts into his throat, releasing a drop of blood that slides over his Adam's apple. 'What was the plan? Thorpe's plan for me?' Carter whispers the words into Epstein's ear. 'The East River? A swamp in New Jersey?'

Epstein can't help himself. He swallows before speaking. 'One bullet, in the back of the head. So the hit would look professional, right? Thorpe wanted you found and linked to Maguire's homicide. That would close the case for my bosses, the media and the public. Everyone gets to go home happy.'

'Except me,' Carter points out.

Epstein doesn't want to be the first to speak, but he can't help himself. 'Don't kill me,' he pleads.

'Why not?'

Epstein's first instinct is to promise that he'll somehow bury the evidence, the DNA and the video tape, but the lie is so transparent he hasn't got the balls to say the words out loud. Finally, he says, more to himself than to Carter, 'I want to see my son.'

'Sorry, but it's too late for that.' Carter's tone is dismissive. 'When you took Thorpe's money, you picked up the gun. You can't put it back down just because you have a family. Your family's why you shouldn't have picked it up in the first place. So, what's Thorpe paying you?'

'Fifty grand, split between me and my partner. It was supposed to be for information.'

'But then Thorpe's scheme encountered this little problem named Carter, this tiny hiccup, and he shifted to plan B. Well, the one good thing about Thorpe is that he's predictably treacherous. I was sitting outside when you and your partner walked up. Tell me how Thorpe keeps in touch with you.'

'E-mail.'

'Has Marginella paid off yet?'

'I don't think so, but how can I be sure?'

'Yeah, that's the whole point with Thorpe. You can never be sure.' Carter pauses, then adds, again with a laugh, 'So long, cop.'

Initially, Solly Epstein maintains control. When he briefs Billy Boyle, while they search for, then find, Epstein's shield and gun in an alley behind the building, as he drives Billy from Astoria to OCCB headquarters on the west side of Manhattan, until Billy Boyle gets out. Then, with no witness to his breakdown, Epstein blubbers his way across Manhattan and Brooklyn, his eyes at times so blurred with tears that he wanders from lane to lane. He's still a mile from home when he pulls to a stop in front of a bar on Eighty-Sixth Street. Inside, he empties his bladder, then scrubs at his face as if trying to erase all memory of Leonard Carter. His skin is red and raw by the time he finally gives up. Epstein wants to know why he's alive. He wants some meaning or purpose to emerge from the experience. But the fear is still too great, the fear that he was about to lose everything in an instant, not only Sofia and Jonathon but the entire universe, every planet and every star, every asteroid, every black hole. Everything in an instant.

A thought emerges from this chaos, a shimmer at the edges of Epstein's mind. He thinks maybe he'll just walk away. Champliss and Radisson won't hold it against him, given Sofia's advanced pregnancy. He can retire to the safety of home and hearth, his life restored.

Epstein laughs out loud. The bosses hold it against him? How about Montgomery Thorpe? What will Thorpe do if Epstein stops delivering? Demand the return of his down payment and be on his way? Or will Epstein become a liability, another Carter? The sad fact is that Thorpe knows a lot more about Solly Epstein than Epstein knows about Montgomery Thorpe. The sadder fact is that Epstein's locked into a fixed address, a sitting duck, while Thorpe might be living on the moon.

This reality sobers Epstein and his eyes are dry when he discovers his wife in bed, sound asleep. Sofia's lying on her side, with her belly facing out, and she does not so much as stir when Epstein enters the room. Epstein kneels on the rug next to the bed and puts his ear to Sofia's belly. The child inside her, Jonathon, is as quiet as his mother.

The sounds of his home settle around Epstein, the refrigerator switching on, the furnace shutting off, the soft hiss of Sofia's breath, the rattling branches of the oak in his front yard. Epstein likes his little house. He likes the life he and Sofia live, a life he can't possibly maintain on a single paycheck, even without considering the baby. Epstein had crunched the numbers right after Sofia became pregnant, concluding that his family wouldn't survive the first year of his child's life without a loan from the Credit Union. And even when Sofia returned to work, a good chunk of her salary would be consumed by the cost of daycare.

Meanwhile, the house needed a new roof, the washing machine barely functioned, the furnace was beyond inefficient and he'd postponed replacing his Toyota's struts a half-dozen times. And there was Sofia's sister, too, with her hand out: 'Help me, help me, help me.'

Epstein has no pity for the likes of Tony Maguire and Bruno Brunale, and he holds OCCB in actual contempt. Early on, when Billy Boyle first outlined Thorpe's blackmail scheme, he'd examined his conscience thoroughly and the bottom line was simple: Fuck 'em. Thorpe wanted the files on a semi-prominent mobster and his known associates. He needed the files in order to formulate a plan of attack that didn't interest Epstein, who wouldn't be responsible for its implementation. Or so he'd told himself, captivated as he was by the prospect of financial gain.

'What's Marginella gonna do, run to the cops?' The question had been posed by Billy Boyle over a lunch in Katz's deli on Houston Street, though the message was from Thorpe. 'Boss, the guy's a sitting duck.'

Seventeen

The powder blue sky beneath which Paulie Margarine pilots his Cadillac is as innocent as the sky painted on the ceiling of Dr Morgan's waiting room. A bitterly cold wind out of the northwest has driven New York's pollution into the Atlantic, leaving the atmosphere crisp and clean. But Paulie Margarine's oblivious. He's recalling Dave Flannery and asking himself a question: if he could do what he did to the Flab and still fall asleep within seconds, how can he cave in to some pussy Englishman?

This is the main reason why Paulie didn't answer either of Thorpe's calls this morning. But there's another reason, another festering sore beneath Paulie Margarine's saddle. The 'suspicious' fire that destroyed Titanic Fencing? Paulie's been assembling a chain of legit business operations for the past twenty years, and not only because he plans to retire. Paulie's watched more than a few of his buddies' transition from flush to broke on the day they were arrested and had to find a lawyer. Driven by necessity, they upped the tempo of their operations, a strategy that usually resulted in a second bust. Paulie's determined to avoid their fate. He plans to make like a boy scout and be prepared when the cops knock on his door, as they surely will. Thus, the attack on Titanic Fencing was an attack on a carefully nurtured strategy. That it should come after he agreed to pay up? There's an arrogance to Thorpe's operation that clings to Paulie's nostrils like a wet fart. The money isn't enough for Thorpe. He's got to humiliate Paulie, too.

Paulie guides his Cadillac around an SUV, a huge Lincoln Navigator traveling well under the speed limit. The SUV has been jacked-up and its body rides a yard above its axles.

Despite the cold, the windows are open, the better to inflict the rap music blasting from the many speakers of the vehicle's mammoth stereo. Paulie's face tingles with each pulse of the bass.

The point, Paulie assumes, is to intimidate, but Paulie's not intimidated. He wouldn't be intimidated if the SUV was filled with black drug dealers out of Brownsville. He certainly isn't intimidated by four white teenagers barely old enough to shave. As he looks from one to the other, he wonders how they'd react if faced with the Flab's fate. The Flab was pretty tough. Toward the end, he wouldn't stop cursing Paulie no matter what Paulie did. But these kids? They'd have crapped their pants before Paulie walked down into the basement.

As Paulie draws closer to Sing Sing and a visit with Freddy, he re-examines his dilemma for maybe the ten thousandth time. He has the wherewithal to put fifty guns on the street, but nowhere to point them. He can't go to the cops, but even if he could, he has no reason to believe they'd be willing or able to protect him. He has the money to satisfy Thorpe, at least temporarily, but he can't bring himself to make the pay off. He's never allowed himself to be strong-armed, never in his life. You might get the best of Paulie Marginella some other way, but if you tried to muscle him, he'd fight until he couldn't fight any more. Then he'd jump you again the next day.

But there's no one to fight, and no one to talk to, either, not in the city. Paulie's afraid to discuss his problem with his closest advisors, men he's known for decades. He's worried about looking weak. And that's another piece of the puzzle. With a single exception, Thorpe has Paulie Marginella totally isolated. The exception is Freddy Marginella. Of Paulie's three kids, Freddy was the one Paulie could talk to. Even if he didn't always tell him everything.

True to form, some half-hour later, seated across from his son, Paulie omits a number of significant details from his tale of woe, like the Flab's demise and the account at Banco de Panama. But he's straightforward about Thorpe's ruthlessness.

'The fire at Titanic, it was like killing a hostage. You know what I'm sayin', right? Keep the pressure on, not to mention turn up the heat. Titanic won't open its doors for six months, even if the insurance comes through. Meanwhile, our customers are searching for new vendors. Who's to guarantee they'll come back? I mean, I forgave a thirty grand debt for a piece of the company and I could end up in bankruptcy.'

Freddy leans forward, his mouth drawn into a frown. 'How'd Thorpe link you to this company, Titanic Fencing? I didn't know myself.'

Paulie Margarine experiences a quick shot of guilt, followed by a sudden insight. Paulie's relationship with Titanic Fencing was known only to Paulie and his legit partner, Milton Fineberg. A connection between Fineberg and Thorpe? Paulie doesn't think so. You'd have to add another step, like Fineberg to the cops to Thorpe. Fineberg's afraid of his own shadow. If the cops threatened him with a racketeering indictment, the fink wouldn't stop talking until they wired his jaw shut.

A smile, the first in days, spreads over Paulie's face. His visit's already paying off. 'I don't know who's ratting me out, and I really don't care,' he tells his son. 'That's because Thorpe already has the information. Even if I eliminate the rat, it ain't gonna solve my problem.'

Freddy takes a moment to consider his father's response, then says, 'If it was me, I'd pay the asshole, then spend the rest of my life trackin' him down. There are people out there who can find anybody. Sooner or later, the jerk'll surface.'

Paulie waves the remark away. This is familiar territory. 'Yeah, fine. Meanwhile, you should watch your back.'

'You think so?'

'Freddy, this guy knows more about me than I do about myself.'

A loud argument between a convict and his female visitor interrupts the conversation. Paulie watches the screws descend on the prisoner. He's wondering if they'll hold back, what with so many witnesses, but they don't. They slam him to the floor, cuff him, yank him to his feet, drag him away. The show's over in thirty seconds.

Paulie and his son observe the performance without changing expression. And they don't comment afterward. Instead, Paulie asks about Freddy's poetry class, then watches his son repress a grin.

'Mr Sandalowsky doesn't like my work, Pop. After I submitted my last poem, he told me not to come back.'

'What was the poem about?'

'About a male hooker with jock itch.' Freddy shakes his head. 'A guy with Sandalowsky's education, you'd think he'd have more compassion.'

Paulie leaves an hour later, stepping through the last of a series of locked doors on to a wind-swept parking lot. The cold slices through his coat and he hustles to his car, his hands jammed into his pockets. Within seconds, his knees begin to ache. Nothing new here. The winters are getting tougher and tougher. But Paulie's feeling pretty good, though he isn't sure exactly why. Freddy has promised to speak to a guy who claims to know a guy on the outside who claims he can find anyone. Paulie's not impressed. Too many bullshitters in prison. Too many bullshitters on the street, too. He'd probably do better consulting a gypsy card reader, the way his wife did. That would be Marie the Martyr, whose psychic failed to predict the stroke that killed her client.

The Cadillac starts right up and Paulie shoves a CD into the player. Roy Orbison doing *Only the Lonely*. He adjusts the heater to blow on his feet and legs, then heads off to the Copperwood Diner on Route 133 for a quick lunch. Paulie doesn't care for the décor, too many hanging plants, or for the twenty-something waitress who introduces herself with, 'Hi, my name is Cindy and I'll be your server.' Paulie gets enough of that in Manhattan. But the eight-ounce sirloin burger is juicy and the fries are crisp, as are the slices of red onion he piles on top of the burger. Even the coffee's halfway decent. Paulie tips well at the end of his meal, going so far as to return the waitress's smile when he tries to stand up and his right knee buckles.

'Are you all right, sir?'

'Never better.'

At the door, Paulie stops to button his coat. His Caddy's at the far end of a large parking lot and the wind, if anything, is blowing harder. Before he can take a step, Paulie's eyes begin to water, blurring his vision. He swipes at his eyes with his sleeve, then lowers his head and limps toward the car. He's halfway across the lot before he notices a man bent over the front door of a Toyota parked beside his Cadillac. The man faces away from him and seems to be trying keys in the door on the passenger's side.

Paulie continues on, wondering if he's interrupted a car thief. Or not interrupted, because the man doesn't turn around until Paulie's within a few yards. Then he spins on the balls of his feet to fix Paulie with a pair of blue eyes as cold and impersonal as the barrel of the automatic he holds in his right hand.

'Here's what you're about to do, Paulie. You're about to open all the doors with that remote, then slide in on the driver's side and put both hands on the steering wheel. And you're about to do it now.'

Paulie's first thought, when he saw the gun, was that his turn had finally come. He was going to die and his main regret was that he'd never have the opportunity to get even. Now he's having trouble assimilating Carter's demands. But somehow, even as his brain spins away, his body gets the point. He slides into the car and his hands find the top of the steering wheel. Only then does it occur to him that murdering Paulie Marginella before he pays up is not in Thorpe's interest.

Carter slips into the back and closes the door. 'Good news, Paulie. You're off the hook, at least temporarily. Thorpe and I, we had a falling out. Now, give me the cell phone.'

'You want my cell phone?' Paulie tries for nonchalant, but his voice squeaks at the end. He's remembering Carter's eyes.

'I want the cell phone I put in your car.'

'What about Thorpe? How will he reach me?'

'He won't, Paulie. That's the point. Now take the cell phone out of your pocket and pass it to me.'

Paulie's not carrying a weapon, but he certainly could be. Carter must know this, but he seems unconcerned. Is he stupid, or at least over-confident? As he hands over the cell phone, Paulie glances into the rear-view mirror to find Carter tucked against the door out of sight.

'Now what?'

'A question. Two, actually.'

'Let's hear 'em.'

'How much will you pay if I take Thorpe off your back, if I bring you his head? Keep in mind, Thorpe's too heavily invested to simply abandon the project. In the very near future, he'll either dispatch another shooter to collect his money, or come himself.'

Now Paulie's all ears, not least because he's got a flesh-and-blood enemy sitting in his back seat. Paulie's had enough of ghosts. And then there's the little matter of 350 grand.

'How would I know it was Thorpe and not some poor jerk you picked off at random? In fact, how do I know that you're not Thorpe yourself?'

Carter drops a photo on the front seat. The photo lands face-up, a matter of pure luck. From where he sits, with his hands firmly gripping the wheel, Paulie can make out a group of soldiers, perhaps a dozen, with their arms around each other's shoulders. In the center of the photo, the head of one individual has been circled. Paulie can't discern the man's features, or even guess at his age, but he grunts in appreciation.

'That Thorpe?'

'Yeah. He's identified in the caption.'

Paulie looks down again, then says, 'What's the second question?'

'How much will you pay if I bring Thorpe to you alive?'

Eighteen

Janie's sound asleep when Carter shows up at four o'clock in the afternoon. She seems at peace and he watches her for a moment before settling into a chair, his attention vaguely drawn to the TV hanging over her bed. The set's tuned to CNN, where John Roberts anchors a regular feature, *This Week at War*. Carter isn't much interested until Roberts leads into a segment about an honor killing in the Kurdish north of Iraq, a Yazidi girl stoned to death by her father and brothers because she was seen talking to a Sunni boy.

Carter asks himself why this item is newsworthy. Honor killings take place in Iraq every day. But the answer is pretty obvious. This particular murder was recorded, either on film or digitally, then sold to CNN. There's even a photo of the girl in better days, a formal portrait with her eyebrows tinted blue, her mouth covered in red lipstick and her face coated with porcelain-white make-up. The girl is lovely, without doubt. Just as, without doubt, her portrait was shown to eligible Yazidi men in order to drive up the bride price. At least before she committed her little indiscretion. Perhaps, if she'd been a good girl, she might have found herself the third spouse of an elderly tribal sheikh. As it was, she became an object lesson for other women.

A moment later, Carter's musings are interrupted by the entrance of a man with a stethoscope draped around his neck. Carter shuts off the TV and introduces himself. This is the first doctor he's come across at Cabrini.

'I'm Jane Carter's brother.' Carter explains.

'I am Doctor Ilgowski.' The man's heavy accent places his origins somewhere in eastern Europe. He's young, in his late twenties at most, with a thick head of unruly brown hair that flops over an already narrow forehead. Although his mouth is little more than a scar between his nose and his dimpled chin, he manages a smile when Carter offers his hand. Doctors in New York nursing homes are paid by the head, no matter how much or little time they spend with a patient, and speed is the name of the game. More than likely, Ilgowski is a moon-lighting resident at a local hospital.

Carter glances at his sister. She's sound asleep. When he turns back, Ilgowski is reviewing Janie's chart. 'I want to speak with you about my sister's –' he searches for the right word, finally settles on prognosis – 'my sister's prognosis.'

'There is privacy issue here.'

'Even though I'm her healthcare proxy?' This is a lie. Janie's religious beliefs preclude the termination of her life before natural death, no matter how great her suffering. But Ilgowski doesn't challenge the assertion.

'There is no recovery from this disease,' he declares without looking up.

'I know that, Doctor. But right now I'm more interested in a timeline.'

Ilgowski begins to write furiously. The interview is nearly over. 'Amyotrophic lateral sclerosis is not amenable to treat-ment. There are no remissions, but there are sometimes plateaus. Your sister is right now in a plateau.' He puts down the chart and turns his eyes to his patient. When he speaks again, his voice is not unkind. 'One year perhaps she will live, or she may decline rapidly. Predicting is not possible. Only I can say that she will not recover.'

Janie awakens a short time later. She asks that Carter read to her, but her eyes close almost immediately and Carter is left with the wheeze of the ventilator for company. Fifteen minutes later, he quits the nursing home.

Carter has no particular destination in mind, but he's not ready to settle in for the night. He walks cross-town, to Fifth Avenue, then turns north. Carter wants company, even the company of anonymous pedestrians. These he finds in greater and greater numbers as he makes his way through the mid-town shopping district to the steps of St Patrick's

Cathedral. At another time, he might be impressed by the cathedral's massive bronze doors and the statuary around them. But on this evening his eyes are drawn to the far side of Fifth Avenue. Set before an office tower at the end of a long promenade, Rockefeller Center's Christmas tree rises seventy feet into the air, its branches flashing lights of every color, thousands upon thousands of them.

Carter is suitably dazzled, as are, he supposes, the gawkers packed shoulder-to-shoulder along the promenade. On a whim, Carter decides to work his way toward the tree. He crosses Fifth Avenue, then slowly edges around and between his fellow pilgrims. The tree at Rockefeller Center is an even bigger draw than Macy's showroom windows and the turnout is impressive, despite the bone-penetrating cold. Carter knows what's coming, the physical contact, the press of bodies. But he persists until his belly presses up against a rail surrounding a sunken plaza with a skating rink at the bottom. Around him, the flags of all the world's nations ripple in a steady breeze. Before him, the great tree blazes away.

Overwhelmed, Carter remains still for several minutes before finally turning his attention to the skating rink where a young skater, a girl wearing a gauzy white tunic over a matching body suit, stands in the center of the ice. Though she is no more than nine or ten, her make-up is thick enough to shame the Yazidi girl murdered by her relatives.

At a signal from a woman at the edge of the rink, cameras begin to roll and the girl begins to skate. Sweeping arabesques at first, smooth, graceful and assured, followed by a series of twisting leaps before she comes to an abrupt stop, unleashing a shower of ice. For a moment, the girl remains stationary, smiling a smile that seems to Carter at once innocent and wise. She's still smiling as she begins to turn, slowly at first, then faster and faster, her elbows tucking into her sides as her tunic and her long black hair billow out. When she finally stops short and raises her arms in triumph, the crowd along the rim of the plaza bursts into applause.

Suddenly, Carter is transported back to Afghanistan, to his first days in-country. He's on a recon mission, tucked into the shadows beneath a rocky outcropping that over-looks a walled compound some fifteen hundred yards away. Carter and a soldier named Martinson. As they watch through binoculars, a boy carrying a soccer ball emerges from one of the buildings, shortly followed by a younger girl. Initially, the children merely stand where they are, seemingly engulfed by the ferocious sun. Then the boy lays the ball at his feet and begins to dribble it across the yard. Nothing grows in the courtyard, not a tree or a bush or a single blade of grass, and the boy kicks up a mini-explosion of dust with each step.

Fifty yards away, along a dirt road, two men sit in a foxhole. The men bear AK47s and RPG launchers. Atop one of the buildings, the largest, a man squats behind a Russian-manufactured PKM machine gun. Snipers wait in the small windows of every building, motionless silhou-ettes who seem as much a part of the landscape as the mud walls that conceal them.

Carter and Martinson have been in place for six hours. In that time, they've observed thirty armed combatants, many wearing the black turban of the Taliban. They've observed six women and the two children as well.

Even a few weeks hence, neither will hesitate. They are fighting a war among the people, a war that cannot be fought without a significant number of the people being killed. That's what Captain Warren told them, way back when they were training at Fort Drum. More to the point, their orders require them to forward the compound's exact location, via satellite, to central command. They're supposed to tell the spooks who dispatched them, *Hey, yeah, you were right. The compound is definitely hostile.*

But they're both green. They're new to the game. And they're not being attacked, or even threatened. They have time to think. At least Carter does. He's thinking that the kids he watches are like kids anyplace, with hopes and dreams that bear no relation to the reality at hand. The boy is six or seven, the girl still a toddler. She chases behind the boy, her excited squealing so loud that Carter hears her voice, despite the distance.

'Maybe we should pull back and radio this in.' Tall and gangly, a string-bean of a man, Martinson has emerged from the hill country in western Pennsylvania to fight for his country.

Carter doesn't reply. Their mission is to rid the country-side of enemy combatants. American soldiers will be coming this way in less than twenty-four hours. So, there's nothing to discuss and he finally transmits the coordinates of every building in the compound. To his surprise, he begins to relax within seconds. He's blown the bridge and there's no going back. By the time the compound is obliterated, some thirty minutes later, he's ready to move on.

Not so Martinson. He lays a hand on Carter's shoulder and they wait until the dust settles, until it becomes apparent that there are no survivors. 'Holy goddamn,' he tells Carter, 'we really done it now. Holy goddamn.'

God-damned. That's what Carter takes with him. Damned by God. And what he understands is that it's possible to do God's work and still be damned by God, that neither good intentions, nor good results, mean a mother-fucking thing.

Nineteen

Carter makes two stops on his way back to Janie's apartment. The first is at an internet café on Avenue B, only a few blocks from the nursing home, where he composes an e-mail. He doesn't rush the process. There's much to consider. For instance, did the cop, Lieutenant Epstein, admit his failure to Thorpe? If not, will the cop make another run at Carter? And what will Thorpe do, now that he's unable to contact Paulie Margarine? Conclude that Paulie's decided not to pay? Or that Carter's meddling? And either way, will he then give up? To Carter, this seems unlikely. But if Thorpe's determined to pursue the matter, will he then ask Epstein to approach the gangster, hoping the cop will make a better emissary than he did an assassin? Or will he come himself?

A sudden irrelevant thought snakes through Carter's mind, breaking his concentration. No more slippage. He's alert and ready. Hallelujah.

Sorry to be the bearer of bad news, but I cannot justify further risk without compensation. Pay up, Monty. And no more crying poverty. You've got your fingers in a dozen pies and we both know it. A debt is a debt.

Carter makes his second stop in a trendy bar on Woodhaven Boulevard, The Tub of Blood Saloon. Carter knows it's trendy because he's been here any number of times and the neighborhood's middle-class. But the joint's tricked out like a skid-row dive. Every item of furniture in the Tub of Blood is mismatched and brutally scarred, and the bar is a thick plank laid across a row of barrels. Chunks of brick lie where they've fallen, on splintered floors, while exposed light bulbs at the ends of dangling black wires provide a suitably dim light.

Middle-aged and thick around the waist, the bartender wears a red bandanna and a t-shirt bearing the likeness of Linda Lovelace, the legendary porn star. His heavy cheeks are covered with stubble and his chest hair rides over the collar of his t-shirt. Two men and a woman play pool on a table laid before an inside wall. They swig their beer directly from the bottle and wear blue jeans torn at the knees, but Carter takes them for dressed-down yuppies. His judgment is instinctive, made before he registers their open expressions, or notes the woman's hand-tooled leather bag or the leather coat she's laid across a table, or a laptop computer tucked into a half-open backpack.

Beyond these four, the Tub of Blood is empty, no surprise because the dinner hour is long past and it's two days before Christmas. Carter finds a spot at the end of the bar furthest from the street and orders a hamburger with a slice of raw onion and a beer. He's come to the Tub of Blood for a barbecued brisket sandwich, the specialty of the house.

Carter's on his second beer, about to bite into his sandwich, when a woman enters. She nods to the bartender, who smiles and nods back, then takes off her coat and drapes it over the bar.

'A mojito,' she announces.

A mojito? At the Tub of Blood? Carter smiles to himself. Like the rest of New York, the Queens neighborhood of Woodhaven is rapidly changing. The Italians and Irish who once dominated are either moving to Florida retirement homes, or are already dead. Their replacements are younger, better educated and far less likely to be native New Yorkers. They're richer, too. In the past decade, real estate values have exploded. Janie's two-bedroom apartment, originally purchased for $30,000 shortly before she came to get him, is now worth half a million. Carter knows this because he's had the apartment appraised at Janie's request. Maybe his sister accumulated a decent nest egg before she was struck down, but the ongoing price of nursing home care is taking its toll. Now there's a fair chance she'll go broke and have to apply for Medicaid. At which point, her assets will be up for grabs.

'Quiet tonight.'

At first, Carter doesn't realize that he's being spoken to. He's focused on eating his brisket without soiling his fingers. Then he slowly turns.

'Sorry?'

'I said it's quiet tonight. Everybody's on the road. You know, home for the holidays.'

'No place like it.' Carter meets her gaze, thinking he might as well get it over with. Most women flinch when they look into his eyes, but not all women. And not this woman. She's short and broad-shouldered, with a square face dominated by a head of wavy hair that hangs to her shoulders. Parted in the middle, her hair is a shade redder than auburn, echoing the spray of freckles beneath her eyes. Sprightly, Carter thinks. Perky. A ball of fire at the office.

'Wait, I have an idea.'

She retreats to a battered jukebox, feeds it a dollar bill, then punches in a few numbers. A moment later, Bing Crosby's syrupy voice pours from the speakers. *White Christmas*, naturally.

'There, how's that?' She winks at Carter and extends a hand. 'My name's Maureen.'

'Leonard.' Carter takes her slightly callused palm. 'What do you do?' he asks.

Maureen hesitates and Carter knows he's been too abrupt. As usual. But he's not surprised when she finally answers. 'I help produce videos for a public relations firm. You know, the glories of coal, how pharmaceutical companies are more interested in your health than making a profit, that kind of thing.'

Carter nods. Most likely, Maureen's earned her calluses lifting weights. Another yuppie trapping, the perfect gym.

Carter nibbles at his sandwich. It's not that he's uninterested, but he definitely has other things on his mind. Still, he plays along. 'Does it bother you?' he asks. 'Lying all day?'

'Yeah.' Maureen accepts her drink, takes a gulp. She turns

to Carter and her words tumble out, the syllables all but colliding. 'I figure that's just the price I have to pay. If you want eventually to produce serious documentaries, which I do, you have to have experience. What I'm doing at CC&G is learning my trade. The way I see it, if I get a little better every day, one day I'll be good enough to give my boss – his name is Crocker, by the way, an asshole of the first magnitude – the middle digit on my way out. Until that time, I serve massa as best I can.'

Suddenly, Maureen grins. 'Besides, what I do, it's just a game. The public knows we're full of shit. You see it in the polls. Most people would rather have a pedophile living next door than an oil executive.'

Carter takes a second before responding. 'What about your co-workers? Are they cynical, too?'

'I can't speak for them. I mean, for what they really think. But in the office, we're strictly orthodox. We don't go negative on the client. Massa wouldn't like that.'

Carter steals another look at Maureen before returning to his food, at her quick smile, at the even teeth she displays, the tip of her tongue. Flecks of amber and gold sparkle in her green eyes.

'You going home for Christmas?' she asks.

Carter finishes his sandwich, wipes his fingers and drops a twenty on the bar. 'That good?' he asks the bartender. When the bartender nods, he finally turns to Maureen.

'I'm already home,' he explains. 'I don't have to go anywhere.'

'Lucky you. I'm from Big Butte.' She cocks her head and grins. 'That's in Nevada.'

'Big Butte?'

Maureen continues on, her words streaming forth like spray from a garden hose. 'Big Butt. That's what we called it when I was in high school, me and the other kids who didn't fit in. Big Butt, Nevada, the butt-hole of America. What you think? What you say? Every syllable's mapped out in advance. Evil government desecrating your sacred liberties. The Jewish lobby running foreign policy. One-worlders persecuting white Christians. We don't take government handouts, but keep those farm subsidies coming. And by the way, if I want to let my steers crap in the creek, it's tough shit on my neighbors downstream. No pun intended.'

Maureen tosses her hair and she hesitates, perhaps waiting for Carter to respond. Then she says, 'Not like New York, where you can say anything, the more outrageous the better.'

'True enough, you can say anything in New York. It's just that nobody listens, or gives a damn. Conversation here is like the traffic. After a while you don't hear it.'

But Maureen shakes her head. 'Take this to the bank, Leonard. If you've got a big mouth, like me, New York is the place to live.'

Carter smiles dutifully. 'So, you're not going home?'

'Just because I'm nostalgic enough to play *White Christmas*, doesn't mean I'm ready to put up with my relatives.' She scratches at her neck with the edge of a polished fingernail. 'There are other things, besides . . .'

Carter wants to get back to Janie's apartment, but he thinks there's a point and that he needs to hear it. 'Besides being a refugee from the butt-hole of America?' he prompts.

'Yeah.' Maureen sips at her mojito. 'Look, I know I'm being a little abrupt, but do you want to have dinner with me tomorrow?' That grin again, mischievous and challenging. 'It's Christmas Eve and all my pals have taken off. I mean, if you're not doing the family thing . . .'

'Give me your address and I'll pick you up.'

Carter's reply is prompt, maybe a little too prompt. Maureen's eyes darken. 'My place is a complete mess,' she says, 'which is what you'd expect, me having three roommates. Also, I have to work tomorrow morning. Why don't we meet at the restaurant?'

'You mean here?'

'I was thinking Osteria del Sol. Do you know the place?'

'Near Forest Park?'

'That's the one.'

'Seven o'clock OK?'

'Sure.'

*   *   *

Carter climbs the nine flights of stairs leading to the roof of Janie's building. He's still breathing easily when he finally comes to a metal door, a matter of some satisfaction. The door opens when Carter pushes the bar release, but when he tries the handle on the outside, it won't turn. As expected, the door opens only from inside and Carter has to place a book between the door and the frame to keep it from closing behind him. Carter's purpose is simple reconnaissance. Know the terrain.

He steps on to the roof of the first of three attached apartment buildings. The buildings run north along Eighty-Ninth Avenue before giving way to a pair of two-family homes. Carter takes a minute to allow his senses to expand, then walks to the nearest building, where he again hesitates long enough to get his bearings. Though Carter's eight stories up and there's a steady breeze blowing out of the northwest, he's not aware of any discomfort.

Carter drops to the roof of the second building some eight feet below. He crosses to the door leading into the building, finds it locked, and continues on, to the third building. Here the drop is a mere yard and Carter steps down on to the roof without making a sound. Again, he approaches the door and tugs at the handle. This time the door opens.

Carter moves to the wall furthest from the street, drops to his knees and looks over the edge, exposing as little of his body as possible. As expected, he discovers an alley bounded by a tall, chain-link fence. The alley runs behind all three buildings to a narrow driveway that leads out to Eighty-Ninth Avenue. On the other side of the fence, the back yards of seven unattached homes span the entire block. Even in winter, the trees and shrubs will provide excellent cover to a man on the move.

Several minutes pass as Carter maps a series of exit routes. He counts seven altogether, through the front and rear of this and Janie's buildings, and down the fire escape of any of the three. The possibilities expand from there and Carter doesn't rush the process, knowing there may come a time when he needs to leave in a big hurry, when he'll have to rely on instinct. Nevertheless, he can't possibly memorize every possibility and he finally drops to his hands and knees before approaching the edge of the building overlooking Eighty-Ninth Avenue. He's on his belly by the time he exposes his head, which is a good thing, because his new friend, Maureen, is sitting behind the wheel of a black Chevy on the far side of the street.

Carter's neither surprised nor disappointed. All along, he's known that he could be tracked to Janie's apartment. But he does have a problem. Long term, he can't just disappear. Even should he desert Janie's apartment, Thorpe will eventually discover the Cabrini Nursing Center. Carter's not ready to desert his sister. Not even close.

Carter steps out of Maureen's line of vision, then begins the last of the tasks he's come to perform. Taking his time, he creates a mental map, noting the location of every rooftop that offers a line-of-sight to the front door of Janie's apartment house. Montgomery Thorpe is a manipulator and a schemer, not a fighter. Should he summon up the courage to deal with Carter personally, he won't confront his protégé. He'll lie in wait.

Back in Janie's apartment, Carter reconsiders a project he's been turning around in his mind for the past month. Carter's dissatisfied with his workout. The Sinawali system is fine for an empty room. But most environments are filled with objects. To be aware of them, to move smoothly between and around them, would be as advantageous as tripping over them would be disadvantageous. How many times had Thorpe lectured him about using terrain to lure your enemy into a trap? Environment is environment, whether it involves armies maneuvering on the battlefield, or two drunks in a back alley.

Carter's wants to remake the larger bedroom, Janie's room, into an obstacle course by arranging tables and chairs in random patterns that he can change every time he works out. But there's a problem. The room is already packed with furniture. There's a queen-sized bed, a triple dresser, an armoire, two nightstands, a vanity, even a chaise lounge.

The furniture is halfway decent, if unexciting, especially

to Carter who's committed to the concept of traveling light. But this is Janie's furniture, accumulated over a lifetime. These are her treasures, from the porcelain ballerina on the vanity to an arrangement of photos on the dresser. Carter's in those photos. Carter and Janie at Jones Beach, in Disneyland, standing at the edge of the Grand Canyon.

Carter opens a closet to find it stuffed with suits, slacks, blouses and sweaters. He knows that Janie will never wear them again. Janie knows it, too. If he means to live in the apartment, he needs to get rid of her clothing and whatever furniture he doesn't want.

But Janie's still alive. She's still alive and she's not about to die any time soon. In Africa, Carter knew men who claimed that spirits resided in the most ordinary objects, in canteens, in binoculars, in the odd bit of jewelry. Carter never bought into their beliefs, as he never bought into the beliefs of the Episcopalian church Janie dragged him to every Sunday. Still, he feels Janie's presence in the apartment, as he smells, faintly, the scent of her perfume on her clothing.

Maybe tomorrow, he thinks. Maybe tomorrow I'll give her clothes to the Salvation Army. Maybe tomorrow I'll be dead.

Twenty

S olly Epstein's day begins on a bright note. He's in the Crime Scene Unit's lab, in the video room, he and Billy Boyle, conferring with Tina Metzenbaum. CSU's techs have been working on the Orchid Hotel video all night and Epstein's anxious to view the results. He's afraid they've gotten Carter right. That would force his hand.

'We went to the computer first,' Tina explains. 'You know, when in doubt, beseech the technology god. The video was analyzed pixel by pixel and a supposedly enhanced image generated. Worthless image is more like it.'

Epstein stares at the glowing face on Tina's computer. The shape of the head is right, and so is the curve of the nose, but the eyes, mouth and chin are little more than vague shadows.

'You can't even tell the guy's age,' he complains. 'He could be anywhere between twenty and forty.'

'That's what we figured, too.' Tina picks up a manila envelope and removes a sheet of paper. 'So we faxed the computer enhancement to an artist, Cynthia Ratigan, a civilian we use for difficult reconstructions. Normally, I don't believe in going outside the job, but this woman's practically psychic. She did a reconstruction from a male vic's skull that was dead-on. We identified him forty-eight hours after her sketch hit the airwaves.'

Epstein fears the worst, but the sketch looks nothing like Carter. Everything's wrong, every feature, even the overall shape of the head. The man in the sketch glares from beneath heavy brows. His mouth is twisted at one end, into something between a sneer and a snarl. Even his nostrils are slightly flared. Meanwhile, Carter's eerie calm was the

scariest thing about him. His voice hadn't betrayed a trace
of anger, or even resentment, at the attempt on his life.

'Let me ask you this, Tina.' Epstein steals a glance at
Billy Boyle. Billy's been quiet all morning. 'When I show
this sketch to Champliss, do I . . . No, scratch that. Just tell
me that CSU stands behind this sketch. Tell me you think
the artist got it right.'

Tina lays a hand on her hip. She's grinning now. 'We
have our own artists, Solly, and we naturally ran the enhancement by them first thing. They couldn't help us. Not enough
detail, they'd only be guessing. So we farmed the job out
to Cynthia Ratigan, who provided this rendering, which I
now pass to the commander of the appropriate task force.
You want more than that, talk to my boss.'

Epstein remains silent on the short drive through the
Midtown Tunnel and on to Second Avenue in Manhattan.
Christmas Eve or not, Champliss wants a meeting in his
office. The news Solly will deliver is anything but good, at
least from his boss's point of view. Not only have they
come up empty on the sketch, but no further tapes have
emerged, despite the Flash's mighty efforts. And while the
presence of mitochondrial DNA has been confirmed, in
order to make a comparison, there has to be a suspect.
Which there isn't and will never be if Epstein has anything
to say about it. Not a live suspect, anyway.

'What we did, Billy, is get suckered.' Epstein's right hand
is inside his coat, stroking his rib cage. He thinks he's
making sure that he's still here, still above ground. He can't
understand why Carter left him alive and he somehow feels
that he doesn't deserve to live. Talk about in over your
head? Epstein feels like he's drowning.

'Just the files on Paulie, right?' he continues. 'That was
the original deal with Thorpe. Then the case falls into our
laps and suddenly we're keepin' Thorpe abreast of the investigation. But even that's not enough, not after the Flash
turned up the heat with that video. Now we're supposed to
whack Carter to protect our own interests. I don't know
about you, but me, I don't like bein' suckered. Especially

by someone I can't find. I mean, Thorpe could be anywhere in the world. He could be right behind us.'

Epstein opens the window, leans out, takes a deep breath. The temperature has been rising since early morning and the air is saturated with moisture. He peers down a mist-shrouded Second Avenue. He notes buildings, stores, heavy traffic, lots of pedestrians – it's Christmas Eve and everybody's going somewhere. There are no icons in sight, no great bridges or skyscrapers, but Epstein's satisfied with the view. Satisfied to be breathing air. Instead of eating dirt.

Billy Boyle pulls over to let an ambulance go by. He turns his dark eyes to his boss. Billy was an MP in Iraq, assigned to guard duty at a number of prisons, including Abu Ghraib. Not that Billy talks about his experience, but Epstein has the distinct impression that his protégé's honorable discharge was more a matter of luck, than discretion.

'This guy, Leonard Carter, I might know where to find him,' Billy says.

Epstein's hand jumps to his knee, which he begins to rub. 'How's that, Billy?'

'I called in a favor from an army buddy, works out of DC now. He took a peek at Carter's service record. Seems that Carter's pre-enlistment address and the address of his next of kin, a sister, are one and the same. You want, we can check it out.'

Billy Boyle eases the department Ford into heavy traffic that will only get heavier as they approach the East River bridges. He drives facing forward, his uneven features composed. Epstein runs his hand along his thigh, from his knee almost to his hip. Billy's telling him that they can track Carter down. He's reminding Epstein that as long as Carter's alive, he's a threat. For starters, he has Epstein's home address and he knows about Epstein's relationship with Thorpe. And there's the other part, too, the personal part Epstein doesn't want to think about. Carter put a knife to Epstein's throat and made him beg. You can't let that ride, not if you're a cop. Not if you're Billy Boyle.

But there's no element here, practical or personal, that Epstein hasn't already considered. And if Carter was some

ordinary gangster, he wouldn't hesitate for a second. But
he's come to the conclusion that Leonard Carter's a freak
of nature. You want to go up against him, bring a SWAT
team.

Traffic slows to a halt as they pass Fourteenth Street. Not
for the first time, Epstein questions the wisdom of locating
police headquarters between a pair of East River bridges
in the heart of Manhattan's financial district. In Brooklyn
or Queens, for the same money, you'd get twice the space.
But the outer boroughs were never in the cards. Lower
Manhattan is the engine that turns the prop that drives the
city. The high priests of the Puzzle Palace could no more
resist its allure than iron filings resist a magnet.

Champliss takes one look at Cynthia Ratigan's sketch and
shakes his head. He lays it on his desk, then picks up a printout
of the computer enhancement. 'What I don't understand,' he
tells Epstein, 'is how you get from this enhancement to that
sketch. I don't understand the process.' He holds up the
enhancement. 'This is nothing. Less than nothing. You
wouldn't be able to recognize the man if he was staring
you in the face. But somehow the artist arrived at this sketch.
How?'

'I don't know,' Epstein admits, 'but we've got another
problem. Ratigan's a publicity hound. She's been inter-
viewed on Court TV several times, CNN, too. If we don't
release the sketch, she might take it to the media on her
own.'

This is an argument Epstein developed on the ride downtown. Epstein wants the sketch released, as he wants the
investigation to go permanently off track, his career be
damned. If released, the sketch will draw hundreds of
responses, each of which the detectives under his command
will have to investigate. By the time they finish, the case
will be stone cold dead.

Champliss draws a hissing breath through his long nose.
He's getting the point. 'Today's Christmas Eve, tomorrow's
Christmas. Nobody's paying attention to the news, on tele-
vision or in the papers. So if we do release the sketch, we

won't do it until Sunday evening. That gives us a few days. You might take the time to pay Ms Ratigan a visit. You might explain the difference between cooperation and confrontation as it applies to the New York Police Department.'

'Like you said,' Epstein responds, 'today's Christmas Eve and tomorrow's—'

'So what?'

Epstein stares at his boss for a moment, trying to decide whether Champliss is making some sort of cop-macho argument. Holidays don't matter, job before family, stiff upper lip. That would be truly amazing, because the way Epstein heard it, Champliss was angling for a desk job before he left the Academy.

'All right, boss. Anything else?'

'Keep your men working. Stick it to them, Solly. Before we decide whether or not to release the sketch, we need to know if there's an arrest on any horizon, near or far. Myself, I don't think the story will die out on its own.'

Epstein's on his cell phone before he reaches the elevators. Baby, baby, baby, baby. Sofia's not happy. No surprise there. Epstein's not all that overjoyed, either. But there's a lot at stake here.

'I only have a few more stops to make,' Epstein explains. 'I'll be home by two.'

'I feel like it's his first Christmas, Solly. I'm talking about our son. I don't want him to spend it alone.'

Epstein lacks the courage to point out any of the flaws in her reasoning. 'I promised to take you to midnight mass at St Patrick's. This is a promise I mean to keep.'

'I truly hope so. Because the way I'm feeling now, I don't want to be alone tonight, either.'

A good shot, Epstein admits to himself. Enough guilt there to last until Easter. 'The faster I get to work, the faster I get home,' he counters.

'Just make it soon. I need you, baby. Our son needs you.'

Twenty-One

Epstein and Billy Boyle make their first stop at the office housing the task force. Epstein's thorough, if a little abrupt. He first reviews each of the victim files with the appropriate detectives. Nothing new, praise the Lord. Then he divides his task force in half, the first half to work Christmas Eve, the second Christmas Day. Their job is to man the hotline from nine to five, and to report any leads to him via cell phone. Epstein doesn't shift blame for this assignment to the bosses. As far as these men are concerned, Solly Epstein's the boss. If they don't like him, tough shit.

By noon, Epstein and Billy Boyle are on the road again, driving north, toward the community of Inwood at the tip of Manhattan. Their route, along FDR Drive, takes them past every tunnel and bridge spanning the East River, and past the George Washington Bridge, which crosses the Hudson. Epstein has Billy Boyle use the siren and the flashing lights in the grill, but their progress is still painfully slow. Epstein might have called ahead, hoping Cynthia Ratigan was out, but due diligence being the order of the day, he wants to claim that he literally knocked on the artist's door.

Ahead, the towers and cables of the Triborough Bridge appear for a moment, a shadow within a shadow, then as quickly disappear as the fog thickens. Epstein's thoughts are mainly of Sofia. He's thinking it'd be real great if he stayed alive. Being as his wife needs him. Being as his son needs him.

'So, Billy, let's say Carter's holed up at his sister's,' Epstein says. 'What do you wanna do about it?'

Billy Boyle replies without hesitation. 'Kill two birds with one stone.'

'Pardon me?'

'I wanna give him to Paulie Margarine.'

Epstein takes a deep breath, then crosses his legs. This is the best idea he's heard in years.

Cynthia Ratigan projects an air of distraction as she leads her guests to a loveseat in her tiny living room. In her forties, Ratigan's blonde hair is short-cropped and mostly concealed by an elaborate silk wrap that seems, what with its repeated geometric figures, vaguely African. The wrap is at odds with her dress, a white kimono sprinkled with lotus blossoms, and with her slippers, too, which are curled at the toes, pixie style. Meanwhile, every finger of both hands, including her thumbs, is circled by at least one ring. Epstein suspects that the rings have some mystical significance, though he's not stupid enough to enquire.

'To what do I owe this honor?' she asks.

'You were good enough to do a reconstruction last night. From a computer enhancement?' Epstein's left hand reaches up to stroke the side of his face. Still there.

'The Macy's Killer. He'll be in my book.'

'Your book?' Epstein asks.

Cynthia reaches into an overflowing ashtray to pluck out a thin, half-smoked cigar. She lights the cigar, then blows a smoke ring at the ceiling. 'I want to share my gift, Lieutenant. And I want to make the world aware of the terrible price to be paid.'

Epstein leans a little closer. 'So, you're sticking by your sketch?'

'My resurrection,' she corrects. 'I speak for the victims, through the victims, and with the victims.'

The wall behind Cynthia Ratigan is lined with bookcases. Epstein glances at the titles as he decides what to say next. The basic question has already been answered, but Champliss virtually ordered Epstein to make a threat on behalf of the NYPD. Something about explaining the difference between cooperation and confrontation.

Epstein registers a few of the books' titles: *Essential Spirituality*, *Messy Spirituality*, *The Spirituality of Success*, *The Spirituality of Imperfection*. He's not encouraged. But then he notes a cluster of textbooks on a bottom shelf, including Caroline Wilkinson's *Forensic Facial Reconstruction*. That's better. Ratigan isn't totally deluded. Or even if she is, she can still claim technical expertise.

'I have a master's degree in forensic anthropology from Boston University.' Ratigan takes another hit on the cigar.

'Is that a question?'

'No, it's an answer. An answer to the question you're too polite to ask. You want to know if I'm full of shit. If I'm making it up as I go along. That's why you're here.'

Epstein smiles. 'You have to admit, there's a lot of empty space between the computer enhancement and the sketch you drew.'

'There is.'

'And there are consequences, too. For instance, if we charge a suspect and your sketch is off-base, the perp's lawyer will use it to prove his client's innocence. He might even call you as a witness.'

A fleshy woman anyway, Ratigan's cheeks explode when she grins. 'Nicely stated,' she tells Epstein. 'Testifying in public on behalf of a guilty defendant would be a uniquely painful experience.'

'That's true. And if the sketch becomes public knowledge, the prosecutor will have to call you, even if the defendant's lawyer doesn't. He'll have no choice, because the jury will want to know how you bridged the gap between a worthless computer enhancement and your extremely detailed portrait. Step by step.'

'And the prosecutor will have every reason to make me look like some kind of hippie asshole.'

'Worse, a charlatan or an opportunist.' Epstein leans forward. 'So, I'm asking you again. Do you stand behind the accuracy of your . . . your resurrection?'

Ratigan brings the cigar to her lips before realizing that it's gone out. She looks at the cigar for a moment, then drops it into the ashtray. 'If the department doesn't have faith in my work,' she quite reasonably asks, 'why did they give me the job in the first place?'

Epstein finds himself growing more and more nervous as he and Billy Boyle approach Jane Carter's apartment house in Brooklyn. He tries to hide his apprehension from his subordinate, but he can't be sure he's succeeding. Billy Boyle's expression never changes, except when he's angry. It's as if he isn't interested in his own life, as if his life runs on simply because running on is what lives do. Billy Boyle has no wife or children, no hobbies, no interests.

As they pull to a stop, Epstein entertains a brief fantasy in which an emotionally disturbed person wearing a Santa Claus hat pushes Carter in front of an oncoming A train. He visualizes every step of the process: the distant roar and rattle of the train as it approaches the station, Carter leaning over the platform's edge, the rush from behind and the shove, finally Carter's flailing hands. Like he's trying to climb an invisible rope.

Billy Boyle opens the door and starts to get out, but Epstein restrains him. 'I'm gonna give Champliss a call, bring him up to date,' he tells Billy.

Epstein wants to add, Why don't you go ahead without me? but stops himself at the last second. More or less resigned, he taps Inspector Champliss's phone number on to the keypad of his cell phone.

'Ratigan's gonna put the sketch in her book,' he tells his boss.

'Her book?'

'What could I say? She considers herself a celebrity.'

'Did you explain . . . ?'

'I did. I described what might happen if her sketch was pure bullshit, the unpleasant consequences. I was very explicit.'

'What did she say?'

'That she didn't call us, we called her. She wanted to know why we'd do that if we didn't have faith in her abilities. Myself, I gotta admit, I didn't have an answer.'

* * *

Epstein snaps his cell phone shut, opens the door and steps into a light snowfall. As he waits for Billy Boyle to join him on the sidewalk, Epstein finds himself wanting to say something. But there's nothing to be said and they walk in silence to Jane Carter's building, where Billy rings the super's bell. A moment later, the intercom to their right emits a burst of unintelligible static. Billy Boyle leans on the buzzer again, holding the button down until a man emerges from a stairway at the back of the narrow lobby. Middle-aged and stocky, the man carries an open-end wrench that has to be two feet long. He's holding the wrench across his chest, but he lets his hand drop to his side when Billy Boyle reveals his badge.

The man's name, it turns out, is Miguel Romero, and his conversation with the two cops is brief. Billy Boyle shows Romero a photo of Carter taken from Carter's service file. The photo is six years old, but Romero doesn't hesitate.

'Tha's Lenny Carter. He moved into his sister's apartment a couple of days ago.'

'Jane Carter's apartment?' Epstein asks.

'Yeah, she's in some kinda home in Manhattan. A nursing home. She's got like this disease. She's like dyin'.'

Epstein thanks the man, then turns to go. But Romero's not through. 'Do I got somethin' to worry about?'

'Yeah,' Billy Boyle says, 'you gotta worry that you'll shoot off your big mouth and the guy in that picture will find out we were here. If that should happen, it's gonna be Abner Louima time in Woodhaven when I shove that wrench up your ass.'

Epstein arrives home, Billy Boyle in tow, at four o'clock in the afternoon. Sofia doesn't much like Billy Boyle, but they need him to sit with the car while she and Epstein attend mass at the cathedral. In the meantime, there's plenty to do. There's a set of outdoor lights for the front door, while the tree, currently in the garage, has to be retrieved, erected and decorated. Here Billy Boyle proves invaluable, working almost by himself, so that Epstein is able to supervise from the couch next to Sofia.

From time to time, when Billy Boyle is distracted, Epstein lays the palm of his hand on Sofia's abdomen. Jonathon is awake; his little fists and heels thump against his mother's belly. Suddenly, Epstein finds himself wondering if Jonathon has any sense of 'out there'. He wonders if birth comes as a complete surprise to newborns. He imagines the pain they must feel as they move through the birth canal. Epstein has assisted at two births in his capacity as a police officer. He's observed the process up close and he knows it can't be any easier for the kid. Intelligent design? Yeah, right.

When Billy Boyle plugs in the lights for the first time, Epstein's heart takes a little jump. He turns to his Sofia and finds her smiling. She lays her head on his shoulder and strokes the back of his hand.

'Jonathon's first Christmas.'

Epstein doesn't argue the point. He loads a CD into his stereo – traditional Christmas carols performed by the choir of King's College in England – and sets the volume low. Then he fetches a bottle of non-alcoholic wine and a bottle of Chivas. Sofia gets the wine, Billy and Epstein the scotch. All appear satisfied with the moment, especially Epstein. As the choir sings the opening notes of *Away in a Manger*, he again visualizes Jonathon's first real Christmas, a tree tall enough to brush the ceiling, presents piled on presents, brilliant red poinsettias on every horizontal surface. He even imagines an enormous stocking hung above a fireplace he doesn't have.

Pleasant thoughts, no doubt, but the realities are not so easily shelved. After a second drink, Epstein's thoughts inevitably darken. He admits that maybe he's already trashed his dreams, that maybe the bullet's already in the air and maybe he's walking right toward it. And for what? For money he's already spent? How stupid can you be? And what was he thinking all those months ago when Billy Boyle first pitched him?

Epstein finally answers this question as he and Sofia listen to the choir at St Patrick's sing *O Little Town of Bethlehem*. He's always liked this particular carol. The hopes and fears of all the years? A lot of weight there. But

Epstein's not listening to the carol. There's another voice out there, far more insistent, a voice telling him that true criminals don't consider consequences, only rewards, no matter how often they're punished. Telling him that's not his fate, no way. If he can just wriggle off this one little hook, Solly Epstein will be a good boy forever.

Twenty-Two

Carter begins his Christmas Eve at 8 a.m. with a stack of pancakes, a half-dozen sausages and a cubed mango. He eats slowly, knowing he probably won't eat again for the next twenty-four hours. Finished, he washes and dries the dishes, then heads off to the living room where he works out for the next hour.

Carter's routine – calisthenics mostly – is necessarily restricted by the heavy furniture, but he makes do. He doesn't think about much of anything as he goes about his business. That's because he knows what's coming and he's not frightened by the possibility that he'll finish second. No, what Carter seeks is focus and his workout doesn't conclude until he finds it, a razor's edge of heightened reality that leaves him as alert as a jack rabbit in a den of rattlesnakes.

Carter's on his way out of the building when he comes upon the super, Miguel Romero, polishing a brass rail in the first floor hallway. Miguel's there to corner residents who haven't yet tipped him. Or so Carter, who's already tightened the man up, assumes. Carter has known Romero for twenty years.

'Merry Christmas,' Carter calls.

'Hey, Lenny, slow up a minute.' Romero waits until he has Carter's full attention. 'Las' night, two cops, they're askin' about you, man.'

'Asking what?'

'They show me a picture, ask if this man lives here.'

'And what did you say?'

'Wha' could I do? If I lie to them, they're gonna find out anyway.'

'And my sister? Did you tell them about Janie?'

'Wha' could I do?'

Romero looks into Carter's eyes, then backs off several feet. But he's reading Carter all wrong. Carter takes out a roll of bills and hands Romero a twenty.

'Did you get their names by any chance?'

'The *maricón* with the fucked-up face didn't say his name. He's jus' tellin' me what he's gonna do if I speak to you. The other one, the older guy, his name was Epstein. I'm thinkin' he tol' me he was a lieutenant.'

Carter hauls his laptop to the Cabrini Nursing Center in a leather backpack. He wants to get right to work, but he hasn't missed a visit with Janie in over a month. Plus, it's Christmas Eve. Carter isn't overly sentimental, but he suspects that Janie, what with her religious beliefs, really cares. And he's right about that. His sister's fully awake when he arrives and her eyes widen ever so slightly when he enters her field of vision. Carter thinks that she'd smile if she could. Nobody wants to be alone on Christmas Eve.

Almost before Carter can say hello, he's interrupted by a nurse's aide, a woman named Camilla. Janie's turn for a wash-up, Camilla explains. So sorry, I'll be as quick as I can.

Carter has been through this before and he quickly retreats to a window at the end of the corridor outside Janie's room. Instinctively, he checks the windows and the rooflines of the buildings across the street for snipers. Only when he's satisfied does he turn his eyes to the many pedestrians on the sidewalks flanking Avenue B. He wants to imagine that all their Christmases are joyous, as he did when he was a child torn by envy. That's not possible any more. Carter's fought in too many wars to believe that calamity is a respecter of seasons. Or that a time of birth is not a time of death for someone somewhere. In fact, Carter's becoming more and more certain that death will visit him before the day is done, that he will be an agent of death, or its victim.

Twenty minutes later, Camilla steps into the corridor. 'Merry Christmas,' she calls.

'Merry Christmas,' Carter dutifully replies before rejoining his sister.

As usual, Carter finds himself initially tongue-tied. What do you say to someone who can't respond, especially when the simple truth is off the table? His salesman bit won't do anymore, that's a given, but he can't stand here for the next two hours with an idiotic grin on his face. Finally, he settles on an incident he witnessed nearly a month before, pretending that it happened on the ride over.

'Check this out. I'm on the bus this morning, the Q11, riding up Woodhaven Boulevard to the J Train. The bus is more crowded than you'd expect and some passengers are actually standing. That's most likely because it's Christmas Eve and everybody's playing catch-up. Anyway, at the stop just past Forest Park, we come up on a woman in a wheelchair, accompanied by a nurse's aide. Now forget about Christmas spirit. When the driver leaves his seat to let down the wheelchair platform, passengers are already grumbling at the delay, especially the ones sitting on the seats reserved for handicapped passengers. The driver, he's probably used to the complaints because he just goes about his business. He lowers the platform, waits for the wheelchair to be loaded, then attempts to bring the platform back into the bus. I say "attempts" because the platform rises about three feet and then stops. Now it won't go either way, down or up, and the poor woman is dangling in her wheelchair, screaming her head off. The driver, he does his absolute best to fix the problem. He presses the button over and over. He tries to yank the platform down, push it up. He even jiggles the wires under the platform. But nothing works and he finally has to call his dispatcher.'

Carter leans forward and narrows one eye, again imagining a smile he cannot see. 'Now, if the passengers were upset before, they went nuts when the driver told them to leave the bus. Yeah, that's right. The bus wasn't going anywhere until a mechanic arrived, so every single passenger had to wait in the cold for the next bus, which would be as crowded as the one they left. Janie, the language was unbelievable. GD this and f-word that. Myself, I felt like getting off the bus was an act of charitable giving, totally in tune with the season. But I have to admit that I was a might peeved when a mechanic showed up five minutes later and fixed the problem within a few seconds. And I was even more pissed when the bus took off with only the wheelchair woman and the aide on board. The man standing next to me was so mad he was shaking.

'"Ya know," he told me, "bein' as we're the one's who pay for the fuckin' gimp ramps, you'd think the goddamned city would have more consideration."'

Carter's hoping to keep the conversation light. He has a lot on his plate. But his sister's not buying. She blinks several times, initiating a conversation. Resigned, Carter dutifully works the alphabet, *A* to *K*, *L* to *Z*. Janie wants him to read from the bible and she's very specific about the book and the particular verses. Carter is required to jump from letters to numbers, then to negotiate the difference between Isaiah 1:5 and Isaiah 15. Progress is slow, but Carter's persistence is eventually rewarded when the details finally emerge.

Nevertheless, as he reads the passage, he finds himself wishing they hadn't.

'Why should ye be stricken any more? Ye will revolt more and more: the whole head is sick and the whole heart faint. From the sole of thy foot even unto the head, there is no soundness in it, but wounds and bruises, and putrefying sores: they have not been closed, neither bound up, neither mollified with ointment. Your country is desolate, your cities are burned with fire: your land, strangers devour it in your presence, and it is desolate, as overthrown by strangers.'

Just what Carter needs. It's like getting a Dear John letter ten minutes before going into battle. Plus, Carter doesn't think Isaiah got it right, not as the lesson applies to Leonard Carter. Even assuming that the 'your country' part refers to the state of his soul, Carter isn't rebelling. And he's not wounded or bruised. And the last time he looked he didn't find any sores. Yeah, Janie wants to believe that 'strangers' have corrupted her brother's essential decency. Janie's been trying to save him for the last twenty years. That doesn't make it true.

Still, Carter has to admit that Isaiah isn't all wrong. Carter's life really is a 'desolate' landscape. The only problem is that he has no desire to change his life. Call it fate, destiny, karma or kismet, Leonard Carter's been paddling down this river for a long time and he likes the view.

Carter decides to ignore the message. He's got a lot of work to do and it's after eleven. 'I have a dinner date this evening,' he tells his sister. 'With a girl I met last night. She's from Big Butte, Nevada. A redhead, with freckles. I think we're gonna have a good time.'

And, oh, by the way, if you never see me again, if Maureen blows my head off, goodbye and good luck.

If Carter had his way, he'd take a cab from the nursing home in Manhattan to the garage that houses his van in Queens. But that's not happening. There isn't a bridge or tunnel in Manhattan that's not choked with traffic. No cabbie would take the fare. At another time, Carter might force the issue, but there aren't any cabs to be had in any event. Everyone, it seems, is going somewhere, including Carter, who trudges off toward the V Train station on Houston Street.

Carter enjoys his walk. There's a tension in the air that he finds attractive, an excitement that cuts through the deepening mist. The children seem unable to contain themselves. Prancing about like fractious ponies, they emit little clouds of steam with every breath. After a month of hype, Christmas is almost here. Carter felt this same tension when he walked into Macy's four days ago. Time at once compressed and expanded, the minutes stretching out into a place beyond measurement.

An hour later, Carter opens the door of the garage where he stores his van. He turns on the overhead light and closes the door behind him. Then he methodically assembles the tools of his trade, including a set of long underwear insulated with goose down. He lays each item in a line on the floor, then twice runs a mental checklist. When he's finally satisfied, he loads his gear into a large backpack and drives to The Open Light, an internet café on Vernon Boulevard in Long Island City.

Except for the freak behind the counter, the café is empty when Carter orders coffee and a cinnamon roll. The freak has three earrings in his right ear and the left side of his head has been shaved to the skin. His neck and forearms are covered with tattoos: Popeye, a heart pierced by a dagger, a shamrock, Goofy wielding a scimitar, an iron cross.

'Hey, what's up?' the freak offers.

This is not the first time Carter's been to The Open Light and the freak has obviously recognized him. But there's nothing to be done. Carter pays the tab and carries his order to a table. A moment later, his back to the wall, he opens his laptop and goes to work.

Over the next two hours, using a variety of satellite mapping services, Carter explores the field of battle. His focus is on the area surrounding the restaurant, Osteria del Sol, where he's to join Maureen at seven o'clock. Carter's specifically concerned with any location offering a clear view of the restaurant's entrance.

Osteria del Sol is located on the bottom floor of an apartment building on the eastern side of Woodhaven Boulevard. The building is seven stories high and part of a larger complex of eight buildings. Though the buildings are set at odd angles, opening unusual lines of sight, none offers a ready position covering every approach to the restaurant. To cover every approach, you'd have to lean out of a window or over the edge of the roof, hold your position until Carter happened along, then fire almost straight down.

But if the eastern side of the Boulevard presents serious drawbacks to even a determined shooter, the western side, flanked by Forest Park, more than compensates. Here, the ground rises sharply to an irregular ridge several blocks long. The ridge is somewhere between ten and twenty feet above the sidewalk. The satellite photos aren't sharp enough for Carter to be more precise, but it's definitely high enough for Thorpe's purposes, and for his own.

What's more, though Forest Park is broken up by tennis courts, ball fields and a golf course, this particular corner is heavily forested, with meandering trails that provide avenues of retreat, as well as approach.

Carter leans back in his chair and sips at his coffee. The timing, he admits, is also perfect. With the winter solstice only two days past, the sun will be a distant memory by four o'clock. Thus the odds against encountering an innocent bystander, given the cold and the mist, not to mention the holiday, are enormous. You could find a cozy spot and wait for hours without being discovered. Which is exactly what Carter plans to do.

'Hey.'

Carter glances at the freak. 'Yeah?'

'You want more coffee, dude?' The freak runs on before Carter can reply. 'Because if not, I'm gonna close up. It's Christmas Eve.'

'No, no more coffee. I'm finished here.'

Twenty-Three

The tiny neighborhood of Woodhaven is separated from Long Island City and The Open Light Café by less than ten miles. Nevertheless, Carter's trip from Long Island City to Forest Park takes over an hour. Carter's not foolish enough to try any of the highways that run through Queens County. On Christmas Eve, they're sure to be packed. His route takes him south on Sixty-Ninth Street, from Queens Boulevard to Metropolitan Avenue, then east on Metropolitan Avenue to Woodhaven Boulevard, then finally to Park Lane South, a residential street bordering Forest Park. Carter encounters unsynchronized traffic lights on almost every block, along with double-parked cars, busses and trucks, but he remains patient throughout, even when it begins to snow. He's been here many times in the past, on his way to battle, and the closest he can come to describing his overall emotional state is purposeful.

With the van finally parked a third of a mile from Osteria del Sol, Carter glances at his watch. Four thirty: plenty of time. He strips, pulls on the down-insulated underwear, then adds a Polartec-insulated jumpsuit and a ski mask before donning his backpack. He arms himself lightly, a Glock 9mm handgun snugged into a large pocket, a seven-inch Marine KA-Bar knife strapped to his right thigh, a small dagger beneath his left sleeve.

Finally, Carter regroups, collecting his energies, restoring his focus. Then he dons the backpack and quickly enters the park, traveling no more than twenty yards before crouching on the far side of a steep hill. There's a bit of light here at the edge of the woods, weak and watery light cast by the streetlamps on Park Lane South. Carter can see perhaps fifteen feet ahead and behind, but the interior of the park is a collection of deepening shadows that he knows to be trees but can't really define. The snow falls around him, light but steady. It sticks on the branches overhead and on the dried leaves that carpet the forest floor, dropping in straight lines through air as wet as the rain forests of Sierra Leone.

Carter works his way through the park in a series of short jumps, like a rabbit moving across a field: stop, check, go. The checking part is about spotting predators before they spot you, and Carter's spotting is accomplished with the aid of an infrared night-vision system. He prefers infrared to the light amplifying devices the army trained him to use. Properly camouflaged, a human being is virtually invisible, even in full daylight. Carter ought to know, given the many hours he spent mastering the art. But the human body gives off detectable heat, and will continue to do so for hours after death. There's no stopping the process. Nor is there any device short of a solid wall that will contain enough human body heat to elude an infrared system.

But Carter's precautions are in vain, as expected, an exercise designed to protect against the smallest of possibilities. Without encountering another warm-blooded animal, not even a foraging squirrel, he arrives at his destination, an elevated knob offering a clear view of the restaurant and the apartment complex across Woodhaven Boulevard.

Carter spreads an insulated ground cloth over the leaves, lies down, finally covers himself with a Space blanket. Designed to reflect eighty per cent of the body's heat, the blanket is finished with a camouflage pattern on the outside. Beneath it, Carter is virtually invisible. True, he gives off a heat signature easily distinguished from the much colder ground. But that signature is very faint compared to the signature given off by a man walking upright. He will not be caught by surprise.

In winter, the mountains of Afghanistan are cold enough to inspire terror. Not so Forest Park in late December. The mid-thirties temperature and windless conditions present no threat to Carter. Not that he's comfortable. Far from it. But the ability to endure discomfort is an accomplishment Carter takes for granted. An incentive, not a drawback.

Remaining alert is another matter, and by far the greater challenge. Carter deals with the time by staying active, as he was trained to do. He first measures the apartment buildings across the street against the images he studied on his laptop. Happily, the templates align as neatly as identical fingerprints. As he suspected, there is simply no way to cover the restaurant without leaning over the edge of the roof, seventy feet above the sidewalk, and firing almost straight down. No sane person would attempt the shot, even if he knew when his target was in view, even if he could overcome the inevitable vertigo. And certainly not Montgomery Thorpe, who never trained to be a sniper and whose marksmanship is adequate at best.

That issue settled, Carter places himself at the center of a circle that must be monitored through its entire arc. He divides this circle into ten segments, five on each side of a ragged diameter that runs along the ridge fronting Woodhaven Boulevard. Each segment has its own landmarks and Carter records these every five minutes when he sweeps the terrain surrounding his position.

The snow stops, then starts again, the flakes larger the second time around. As the dinner hour approaches, the traffic on Woodhaven Boulevard gradually diminishes. Virtually every window in the apartments across the way is brightly lit. When Carter sweeps the front of the buildings with binoculars, he spots dozens of Christmas trees, and even a few menorahs. But when he sweeps the forest, only once does his eye settle on a living creature, a dog with his nose to the ground. The animal zigzags across the stunted winter grass at the edge of a pond before disappearing over a small rise. The heat of its body remains behind, a silvery ghost-trail that lingers for minutes.

Maureen shows up at ten minutes before seven. Carter spots her car the minute she turns on to the block, but initially pays her no mind. Instead, he searches the buildings across the street with binoculars, then sweeps the forest behind him with the infrared system. The forest remains dark and cold, the rooftops free of silhouettes. Even the vehicles parked on either side of the road pass an infrared inspection. The only heat rises from the roof and hood of Maureen's car, and from Maureen herself as she strides across Woodhaven Boulevard, then disappears into the restaurant.

Fifteen minutes pass without incident and Carter again settles beneath the blanket. He's thinking that maybe Thorpe plans to take him as he exits the restaurant. That hope buys him a half-hour, until Maureen reappears. She pauses just long enough to look up and down the empty street, then marches to her car and drives away. Again, Carter searches the terrain, but if there's a threat, he can't find it.

Resigned, though disappointed, Carter returns to his own vehicle. He maintains a careful watch as he goes, taking his time, but he encounters no threat along the way, only a man walking his dog on Park Lane South. The man walks with his head down and his shoulders hunched. If anything, he looks even more bedraggled than his soggy Weimaraner. Carter starts the van, makes a u-turn and heads for Woodhaven Boulevard. He's listening to his divided mind, as he might listen to a group of pre-schoolers arguing about the rules of a game nobody knows how to play. There's a part of him that judges Maureen to be an innocent, that judges Carter to be a complete asshole for missing still another opportunity to join the human race. This argument is aided by loneliness, an emotion Carter hasn't felt in years but which now cuts into him like the neck of a broken bottle.

But there's a second voice, too, this one devoid of emotion. Its message begins with an image: Maureen parked at the end of his block, watching his apartment. Innocence? That's like assuming the Iraqi running toward you with an AK47 in his arms is hunting turkeys. No, there's a bottom line here and it's about slippage.

Carter turns into a side street, pulls to the curb and shut off the lights. Always assume the threat. That was one of

Thorpe's many mantras. No matter how peaceful, how friendly the natives, always assume the threat. What was accomplished tonight? By the enemy? The answer is simple enough. The only advantage gained was the knowledge that Carter would be out of his apartment at a certain time. If not to share a dinner with Maureen, then to confront the threat she represents.

Control the battlefield. Another of Thorpe's maxims. Lure your opponent into an untenable position, then attack. Carter closes his eyes. While he was on the rooftops of the three apartment buildings on Janie's block, he'd marked every position offering a clear line of sight to his door. Now he asks himself where he'd wait if he was intent on murdering himself. The first place that comes to mind is the roof of a three-story commercial building, a furniture warehouse on Myrtle Avenue, maybe 200 yards away. The rooftop provides a view, not only of the door, but of Janie's front windows. Given the visibility and the distance, the shot would be anything but easy. Nevertheless, this is a shot Carter would take without hesitation, knowing his target would have to stop long enough to insert a key and open the door.

There are other possibilities as well, from the yards of the one- and two-family homes across the street. Or there might be someone inside Janie's apartment, already waiting. But even so, the warehouse, furthest away, is the obvious place to start. On Christmas Eve it will be entirely deserted.

Five minutes later, Carter parks the van behind the warehouse and a block down the street. The warehouse is now between him and Janie's apartment, where any shooter's attention is sure to be focused. Still, Carter moves quickly, remaining close to the building's façade, until he comes even with a dumpster parked behind a chain link fence. The fence seals off a small parking area just beyond a pair of shuttered loading bays.

Though topped with barbed wire, the fence is no real obstacle to Carter. He's more concerned with attracting the attention of the homeowners across the street if he decides to climb it. But he's not exactly inconspicuous where he is.

Restless, he subjects the warehouse roof, the edge closest to him, to an infrared inspection, but finds nothing. Nor, when he takes a closer look, is there any entrance to the building except through the loading bays.

On the move again, Carter hugs the building as he travels three-quarters of the way around, past the main entrance in front, to a side door. He feels a brief exultation when he tries the knob of this door and it turns freely. Carter's thinking he could move the van on to the block and wait for somebody to come out. He's thinking that would be the safest approach. But Carter's had enough waiting. Plus, he wants time alone with the shooter. There's a message to be sent, after all. He pushes the door open, glimpses a stairway only a few feet beyond, then steps inside. When he closes the door behind him, he becomes functionally blind. There are no windows. He might as well be inside a cave.

Carter places the infrared unit to his eye and scans the stairway, detecting a trail so faint it might be no more than wishful thinking. But he is certain of one thing: no threat awaits him at the top. Carter lays a finger against the wall to his left, then takes a step. The riser is concrete. It neither creaks nor groans beneath his weight.

Reassured, he climbs to a small landing on the second floor and searches it with his hands, very gently, his touch light enough to be the touch of a lover. He discovers a pair of doors and a second flight of stairs. Again, he scans the entire space, including the steps, and again detects no sign of an enemy.

Carter takes a step, then another, then pauses to scan ahead. He can see a faint light at the top of the stairs, but no heat signature. Slowly, he advances, doing that rabbit in the meadow bit – climb, stop, check, climb – until his head rises above the top step and he discovers the source of the light. Carter is staring into a loft that covers the entire floor. Broken by two rows of pillars, the loft is packed with bedroom furniture arranged to create little rooms. Bed, nightstand, dresser, armoire, sometimes an ottoman or a chair. The light bleeds in through six tall windows that face the streetlamps on Myrtle Avenue, so dim it barely kisses the furniture. But Carter's pupils are fully dilated and he discovers the anomalies within seconds: a tall armoire pulled into an aisle, a damaged skylight directly above, broken glass on the floor.

His path decided in an instant, Carter moves into gear. He climbs the last few stairs, slips across the room to the front wall and positions himself behind a second armoire. He slides the Glock into a pocket, then withdraws the combat knife from its sheath. His strategy is based on an old saw: what goes up must come down. And the only way down for anyone on that roof is through that skylight.

So, Carter waits, as he's waited so often in the past, but this time, knowing his enemy's position, he indulges himself. He allows his thoughts to drift back to an operation conducted in Liberia, an ambush that broke the back of a warlord named Tamba Youboty, while incidentally liberating the hoard of diamonds Tamba was transporting to the Congo.

Along with two other men, Jerzy Golabek and Paul Ryan, Carter was stationed on a rock-strewn hillside overlooking a tiny village in the Nimba Mountains. Another eight men were concealed on the far side of the village, in a bend of the only road. The village itself had been abandoned long before, another victim of Liberia's endless civil war. The roofs of the few substantial mud-brick buildings lining the road had collapsed and there were gaping holes in the outer walls.

Positioned in deep shadow, Carter and his companions went unnoticed when Youboty led his boy soldiers, perhaps thirty strong, into the village. Youboty wore a soiled khaki uniform with gold epaulets and a sweat-soaked officer's cap. Jammed into a little parade of technicals, his soldiers wore ragged t-shits and shorts. A few were obviously wounded and many went barefoot. They'd been running for the better part of two days, running from Togaba Kpangbah, the warlord they stole the diamonds from, and they were clearly exhausted. Perhaps that's why they initially failed to react when the first mortar exploded in the center of the convoy.

Going in, the hope was that Youboty would gather his soldiers and retreat along the only road, that he'd run headlong into the larger, more heavily armed force on the other side of the village. Instead, Youboty was killed by the initial mortar round – a matter of pure luck, and not good luck at that. Leaderless, the boy soldiers finally scrambled behind the walls of the little houses when Carter and Ryan open up with their M16s. The engagement would be protracted.

To Carter's right, Jerzy Golabek, formerly of the Stasi, the East German Secret Police, fired off one mortar round after another. The result was predictably devastating, since the buildings that shielded the boy soldiers lacked roofs. At that point, as any trained soldier would know, the boys had two reasonable choices. They could assault Carter's position or they could get their asses in the wind.

But the boy soldiers hadn't been trained to do anything but kill. They chose a third course, one that bordered on collective suicide. Two or three at a time, they dashed into the open, firing RPGs on trajectories more likely to bring down an orbiting satellite than to impact Carter's position.

Carter was too busy killing these children to wonder about their behavior. He was firing off three-round bursts, taking the boys out almost as soon as they appeared. But later on, as he walked among the dead, he tried to imagine what they were thinking when they exposed themselves. Were they merely displaying courage, a kind of ultimate macho? Or did they believe they were protected? Each and every boy had a pouch hanging from a thong around his neck. The pouches contained some sort of vegetable matter glued together with dried blood. Carter knew the boy soldiers were told that these pouches would protect them. But had they really believed it? Had they run into the road thinking themselves invulnerable? Didn't they know their spirit-gods had already been defeated by the bombs and the bullets of men who believed only in the god of money?

Carter is still pondering these questions when a leg drops down through the skylight. In an instant, the past slips from his mind, the shooting, the bodies, the reek of blood and offal. Carter has no room for killings past. The questions he'd asked himself were stupid anyway. War on the ground is kill or be killed. Everybody knows that. Except for boy soldiers.

Twenty-Four

Paulie Margarine is in his hot-tub when his doorbell rings at eight o'clock on Christmas morning. Paulie's got one of the hot-tub's jets aimed at each of his bad knees, which have been aching all night. Lee Pho sits behind him, massaging oil into his back. There's bath oil in the water, too, jasmine scented. Dry skin is another of Paulie's age-related problems.

'Who the fuck is that?' Paulie asks.

Lee Pho doesn't answer. No surprise, as she speaks only a few words of English. The doorbell sounds again, four notes, *ding-Dong-ding-Ding*.

'Jesus Christ,' Paulie mutters.

'Burrday.'

'What?'

'Jee-cry burrday.'

'Yeah, Jesus Christ's birthday.' Paulie stands up, the process divided into segments, neck, shoulders, back, ass, legs. When he finally steps out of the tub, Lee Pho is waiting, towel in hand. He shakes her off and the bell rings again. Faintly, he hears somebody shout, 'Police, open the door.'

On Christmas Day? Paulie thinks. They come for me on Christmas Day?

Paulie shrugs into a terrycloth robe and ties it across his body. Not that he's shy. In fact, there's nothing he'd like more than to wave his dick in a cop's face. Or he would if he was twenty years younger. Now he's embarrassed by the flab around his waist and the loose skin beneath his triceps. Not to mention that his balls hang halfway to his knees.

Paulie reaches the door before the bell sounds again. He peers through the little window to discover a pair of cops on his doorstep, the one from Bruno Brunale, Lieutenant Epstein, and a younger, lumpy-faced cop wearing an expensive coat. To Paulie, this is good news. If they intended to arrest him, they would've brought enough manpower to patrol the southern border. Not to mention a hundred reporters.

'What do you want?' Paulie shouts through the glass.

'Open the door,' Epstein says.

'I'm gonna call my lawyer.'

'Don't do that.'

'Why, you got a warrant?'

The younger cop finally gets in on the act. He draws his weapon and aims it through the window at Paulie's face. 'Open the fuckin' door,' he says.

Paulie obeys without hesitation and the cops walk in just as Lee Pho, fully dressed, makes an appearance. Fortunately, the lumpy-faced cop has stashed his gun. The neighborhood is strictly middle-class and Paulie doesn't need some Korean whore screaming her head off as she runs down the street. He fetches Lee Pho's coat and ushers her out.

'OK,' he tells the cops, 'you muscled your way into my house on Christmas Day. So, whatta ya want?'

They're clustered, the three of them, in a small foyer. Paulie's blocking the way and he's already decided that he's not going to move. Whatever the cops intend to do to him, they'll have to do it here.

'Relax,' Epstein says. 'We're the wise men from the East. We bear gifts.'

Paulie looks from one cop to the other. He's thinking that these are the cocksuckers who fed information to that crazy bastard. The one who jumped him outside the Copperwood Diner. He's thinking that maybe, down the line when they've forgotten all about him . . .

'Last time I looked in the bible,' he says, 'the wise men didn't threaten to blow Jesus's head off.'

'What could I say? It's an updated version. We're makin' allowances for the culture.' Epstein shoves his hands into his pockets. 'All right, no more bullshit. I wanna get back home. I got a pregnant wife. The name of the man who

killed Brunale and the rest of them is Leonard Carter. I
have his address, too.'

Paulie memorizes the address as Epstein reels it off. 'Why
are you tellin' me this?' he asks. 'What's your stake here?'

But the questions answer themselves. He's talking to
a pair of bent cops and Carter knows enough to put them
away. Carter's a problem and Paulie Marginella's the solu-
tion.

'The man's a cold-blooded murderer,' Epstein explains.
'Murder is what he does. It's all he's ever done. If we had
enough on him to make an arrest, he'd already be in custody.
But we don't, so we're giving you a heads-up. What we
figure, even a mutt like Paulie Margarine has a right to
defend himself.'

Paulie manages not to laugh in the cop's face. He even
conjures a smile as he opens the door. 'OK, you made your
point. If there's nothing else, Merry Christmas to you and
your pregnant wife.'

An hour later, Paulie enters the Church of the Immaculate
Conception where he attends mass almost every Sunday. A
number of the Catholics in his crew occasionally show up
at Immaculate Conception. Bruno Brunale was a regular,
along with his wife, Jennifer, and their two children.

As planned, Paulie seeks out Jennifer Brunale and the kids
before taking his customary seat at the back of the church.
This is the first opportunity he's had to offer his condolences
and he goes on for some time, praising his associate's many
virtues.

'Any news from the city?' he finally asks. 'About when
they'll release the body?'

Jennifer Brunale is fifteen years younger than her dead
husband, in her early thirties and drop-dead gorgeous. Paulie
looks into her blue eyes and discovers . . . encouragement,
at the very least. Jennifer Brunale's never worked a day in
her life. No reason to start now.

'One minute they tell me a week, the next they tell me
two weeks.' Jennifer shrugs her well-toned shoulders. 'My
lawyer says there's nothing we can do.'

Paulie responds with his wisest, fatherly-don smile. 'I want you to send Bruno to Calabrasso's Funeral Home on Ditmars Boulevard. Make whatever arrangements you want and tell the old man that I'm good for the tab.'

Jennifer cups Paulie's hand between her gloved palms. Her fingers curl around his. 'Thank you, Paulie, thank you,' she says.

'Hey, Bruno was a good man. I want to lay him out right.'

And bury the jerk is all Paulie wants to do. There's an official version of the attack on Paulie's crew making the rounds: the Flab was responsible, he paid the price in spades, now it's back to business. Needless to say, there's no role for Leonard Carter in this bit of fiction. Better his name should never be mentioned.

Paulie takes his seat just as Father Zambinne approaches an altar virtually buried in flowers. 'The Lord be with you,' he tells his congregation.

'And also with you,' the congregation, including Paulie Margarine, responds.

After mass, on his way upstate to visit his son, Paulie begins to relax. He no longer has to watch his back and he's more relieved than he'd care to admit. The business with Bruno Brunale? Paulie was only inches away when Brunale took a bullet to the head. The shock of it, coming out of nowhere, not to mention the threat to his livelihood, not to mention the cocksucker getting away clean . . .

Well, it's over now, and Paulie feels safe enough to consider a family matter as he pilots his Caddy through heavy traffic on the Taconic Parkway. He's wondering if either of his other two kids, Mike and Rebecca, will give him a call, what with it being Christmas. Paulie's a grandfather who's never seen his grandchildren and probably never will. Neither of his children plan to come to New York and nobody's inviting him to visit.

Paulie doesn't like the fact that his kids are ashamed of him. No father wants that. But their judgment isn't the worst of it. No, with Paulie it's more about the money. Rebecca became a lawyer and Mike became an accountant, with

Daddy paying for every credit. To Paulie's way of thinking, if they wanted to be rid of him so bad, they should've left home when they graduated high school. They should've made their way on their own.

Paulie carries these thoughts into a crowded visiting room at Sing Sing. He and Freddy, the good son, are sitting almost knee to knee.

'What really busts my balls about the situation with Mike and Rebecca is the bullshit,' Paulie explains. 'I mean the bullshit they tell themselves. You know what I mean, right?'

'Pop, I don't have a clue.'

'Mike and Rebecca, they think they're such fine, upstanding citizens. A lawyer, an accountant with an MBA? I wouldn't be surprised if they belong to country clubs.' Paulie leans a bit closer. 'Other kids, they graduate with enough debt to keep them scrabbling for ten years. Mike and Rebecca put their salaries in their pockets from day one. All because of our thing, Freddy, our fuckin' thing. Without our thing, they would've been lucky to graduate from community college.'

'OK, I hear what you're sayin'. But guess what? They didn't send me Christmas cards, either. Ya know, when I first went inside, I wrote Mike a couple of times, but he never answered. Same for Rebecca. Personally, I don't give a shit. What I say to that is good riddance.'

Paulie Margarine shakes his head. Freddy's even-tempered and that's fine. But he's still got a lesson to learn, a lesson about respect. You can't allow yourself to be insulted. Plus, there's the money. Paulie invested nearly a 150 grand in his kids' educations. He's entitled to a return.

'What I think,' he tells his son, 'is that I'm gonna take a trip out to the coast. Now that Rebecca and Mike are in the chips, there's no reason they can't pay me back.'

The sun has already set by the time Paulie approaches the address supplied by Lieutenant Epstein. Leonard Carter's address. He's not surprised when Carter steps out of a doorway before he gets within fifty yards. Nor by what Carter tells him.

'You understand, if you've got backup waiting in the wings, I'll kill you before they get to me.'

'No backup and I'm not armed.'

Carter frisks him anyway, frisks him thoroughly, right then and there. But, again, Paulie's not surprised. In fact, he's pleased. 'Could we go somewhere and talk?'

'Sure, I'll make you a cup of coffee. In fact, it's already brewing.'

'That'd be great.'

Paulie allows himself to be led into Carter's apartment. He's surprised by the homey touches: hand-crocheted throw pillows, a knitted shawl draped over the back of the couch, a crystal vase on the dining room table, the heady odor of brewing coffee. Paulie would never have taken Carter for the domestic type and he figures the apartment is borrowed.

'Take a seat and I'll get the coffee. How do you like it?'

'A little milk, no sugar.' Paulie closes his eyes for a second when he sits down. 'Man, that feels good. My knees are killing me.'

'Fish oil,' Carter says from the kitchen. 'I hear fish oil is good for the joints.' A moment later, he reappears with two cups of coffee. He sets one cup on the end table next to Paulie and carries the other to a facing chair. 'And by the way, Merry Christmas.'

'Yeah, Merry Christmas.' Paulie sips at his coffee, an impeccably brewed French roast. More homey touches. 'So, you gonna ask me?'

'Ask you what?'

'How I found you? What I'm doing here by myself? Why I don't have you fuckin' whacked?'

'The cops gave you my address, Epstein and his partner. You're here because you want to talk about something private, most likely a business proposition.' Carter stirs his coffee, moving the spoon in precise little circles. 'As for why you don't have me whacked? Paulie, if I even smell a threat, I'll kill you.'

Paulie takes a minute to calm down. He tells himself that

he deserves the response, that he shouldn't have asked the question if he didn't want an answer. Carter's not challenging him. Carter's only stating the obvious.

'That thing you did in Macy's, you know, with Tony, it was beautiful,' Paulie finally says. 'How many people you think were in the store?'

But Carter's not about to be drawn into a friendly conversation. Nor is he prepared to admit to a murder. He sets his coffee cup on a table in front of his chair.

'You want to get to the point?' he asks.

'A man of few words? That's good. I like people who know when to keep their mouths shut.' Paulie straightens in the seat. 'Tell me something. Now that your deal with Thorpe is blown, what are you gonna do?'

'I don't know. Money's not something I need to worry about right away.'

'See, that's where you're makin' a big mistake.' Paulie Margarine's tone is almost paternal. 'Everybody needs a life plan. You don't have a life plan, you get knocked around by any wind that happens to blow. You lean this way, that way. It's like trying to find an address without directions or a map. I saw that in a Samurai movie.'

Paulie stares at Carter, who says nothing, though he smiles faintly. 'Anyway,' he tells the younger man, 'I've got a proposition for you, something to think about. Now, I haven't worked out the details, but when I look at you and what you've done in the past few weeks, I gotta think you're a natural. This is what you were born to do. I won't say the word out loud because I know you don't wanna hear it. But this is you, this is your thing.'

Carter has heard this story before. From Montgomery Thorpe. But he's still intrigued. And it's nice to have some company on Christmas Day. He's honest enough to admit that, too. Nevertheless, when he finally responds, he doesn't address the issue of his vocation.

'You don't have to spell out my end of the deal, Paulie. Just talk about yourself. What's your contribution?'

'I'd be your agent.' Paulie rubs at his knee. 'I mean, there's always been a demand for out-of-state talent and I have contacts across the country. I can get the jobs, you can do your thing. What's not to like?'

'Contacts, huh? And exactly how would you contact me? When it was time for me to do my thing?'

'What would make you comfortable? What works for you?'

'E-mail. No contact other than that. No phone number, no address.'

'What about payment?'

'You do the collecting and wire my end to an account somewhere offshore.'

Paulie shifts in his seat, clearly uncomfortable. 'Computers, you know, they like remember everything, even when you tell them not to. I mean, that's the first thing cops do when they get a warrant. Seize your computer.'

'Maybe so, but if you encrypt the hard drive, seizing the computer won't help them.' Carter suddenly rises. 'Now, before we talk money, there's something I want to show you. In the kitchen.'

Yeah, Paulie thinks, like where you keep the knives. But knives or not, Paulie hauls himself to his feet and follows Carter. Paulie isn't kidding about the demand for Carter's services. In Paulie's opinion, most contract killers are complete knuckleheads. Their idea of technique is pulling up next to the target at a traffic light and blasting away. Carter is different. Carter is a skilled professional whose services will definitely command a premium.

'So,' Paulie asks, 'what do you wanna show me?'

Carter opens the freezer door to reveal the head and hands of Montgomery Thorpe. 'Well, as long as you were nice enough to stop over, and as long as we're talking about jobs in the future, I was wondering how much you intend to pay me for this little job I did in the recent past.'

Paulie's dumbfounded. The shriveled gray skin, the crystalline frost gathered at the eyes, nostrils and mouth, the frozen blood around the edges of the wounds – it's too much to absorb at first. Even for Paulie Margarine.

'I hoped to bring him to you in one piece,' Carter finally explains, 'but he refused to come quietly.'

Though Paulie doesn't laugh, Carter's little joke sobers him and he takes a moment to weigh his options. They're talking money, after all. Paulie turns away from Thorpe's remains to look into Carter's eyes.

'Five grand. That's my best offer.'

'You expect me to do "my thing" for five thousand dollars? At that rate, I'd have to perform twenty things a year just to pay the rent.'

With no ready answer, Paulie looks back at Thorpe. The man's eyes are wide open. They're the eyes of a man who saw it coming. 'Hey, blame yourself. When you burned down Empire Fencing, you crippled me. Now I got a negative cash flow that's gonna take a year to reverse.'

Paulie folds his arms across his chest, a gesture designed to indicate finality. But Carter's not biting. He remains silent until Paulie's forced to speak.

'OK, ya prick, seventy-five hundred. But that's as high as I'm goin'. Now, what are we gonna do about them two fuckin' cops?'

Twenty-Five

S olly Epstein is sitting in his living room when his cell phone rings at six o'clock in the evening. Sofia is snuggled up against him with her hands cupped beneath her swollen belly. The presents have been exchanged, Christmas dinner consumed and the dishes washed. It was Epstein who prepared the meal – roast suckling pig – with his wife supervising from a well-padded rocking chair. Ordinarily, Epstein's domestic skills are limited to scrambled eggs and spaghetti sauce poured from a jar. But the little pig had emerged from the oven perfectly cooked, the skin crisp and the meat falling from the bone.

'Do you want to share the brains?' Sofia had asked from her side of the table.

'Nah, you can leave my portion for Santa Claus.'

'Santa came last night.'

'Then how 'bout the Easter Bunny?'

After dinner, they'd retired to the bedroom, Sofia in search of a nap, Epstein in search of a little comfort. Talk about a rough week. Epstein felt like he'd been run over by a dump truck. And the game was by no means over. Having experienced Carter's skills first hand, Solly Epstein has no faith in Paulie Margarine's ability to overcome them. Most likely, the gangster is going to wind up dead. And then . . .

Epstein checks his phone's caller ID screen before answering: 'PRIVATE NAME/PRIVATE NUMBER'.

'Solly, it's Christmas.' Sofia knows that her husband gives his cell phone number to his snitches. 'Don't answer it.'

Epstein wants nothing more than to comply, wants it like

he wants to find his dick still attached when he takes a leak in the morning. Talk about your bad feelings. But it's those same bad feelings that force his hand. Solly's always been a proactive guy. Head in the sand is not his game.

'What?' he growls into the phone.

'You know who this is?'

'Yeah, Paulie, I know who this is.'

'Don't say my name on the fuckin' phone.'

'OK, let's use codenames. I'll be Mr Wolf and you'll be Mr Lion. How's that?'

'You laughin'? You havin' a good time? Because me and you, we got a mother-fucker of a problem.'

Epstein looks at Sofia and shakes his head. 'Before I ask you what it is, tell me how you got my number . . . Mr Lion.'

'You gave me your card, remember? At that thing with Bruno. Anyway, I'm not talkin' on the phone. We got a problem could bury the both of us and you gotta come out here and fix it.'

'Paulie, it's Christmas.'

'Didn't I just say not to call me by my name?'

Solly holds the phone away from his ear for a few seconds. A single evening of peace? With his wife and the child she carries beside him? Call him unreasonable, but one peaceful night doesn't seem like too much to ask.

'Like I said, it's Christmas, so you're gonna have to be a lot more specific. Otherwise, I'm gonna stay right where I am.'

'Specific? On the goddamned phone? You gotta be crazy. Look, I'm at that address you gave me, dealing with a problem you dropped in my lap. Now it's your turn to get involved. If you're too chicken-shit to come alone, call your partner. He's got balls enough for the both of ya.'

Epstein takes Paulie's advice. Over Sofia protests, he dials Billy Boyle's number. Billy arrives an hour later. He wishes Solly and Sofia a Merry Christmas, then lapses into silence. For Solly, it's not that simple. He and Sofia were married three years ago and they lived together for two years before that. These days, he can all but read her mind.

She's telling herself that it's Christmas and she's nine months pregnant and her husband was utterly relaxed until he got a phone call. Now, he and Billy Boyle are running off to God-knows-where, to do God-knows-what. She's telling herself that this is not the Solly Epstein she married.

'I'll be back in time to tuck you in.'

Epstein clips the holster cradling his Glock on to his belt. He wants to add something, but his mind has already turned to the problem at hand. Nevertheless, he pauses long enough to sweep the living room after he kisses Sofia goodbye. Epstein has always been proud of his Ethan Allen furniture, and never more so than now. True, the price tags had nearly blown him away on that particular shopping expedition. One look and he'd suggested a short ride to Macy's. But Sofia had been adamant.

'This is for life,' she'd insisted.

Now Epstein admits she was right. The sofa and chairs, the cherry end tables, the delicately-patterned Aubusson knock-off, the wall unit holding his books, his television, his DVD and CD collections – it all works for Epstein. It works and it strengthens his resolve. Fuck Paulie Margarine. And Carter, too. The NYPD is the biggest gang in New York. The NYPD takes shit from nobody.

Yeah, right.

Epstein and Billy Boyle drive east on the nearly deserted Belt Parkway. The night has turned sharply colder and the skies have cleared. Epstein can see enough stars above the dark waters of Lower New York Bay to imagine whole constellations. Almost at the horizon, two ships stand at anchor, a freighter and an oil tanker, their superstructures ablaze with lights. A sickle moon hangs between them, point down, as though preparing to slice them in two.

'You got vests in the trunk?' Epstein asks Billy Boyle.

'Yeah.' Billy Boyle eases off the gas. He doesn't look at Epstein when he adds, 'I don't like this any more than you do.'

Epstein knows the vests won't stop the bullet that took out Bruno Brunale, knows also that Carter will anticipate their wearing vests and take appropriate measures. Nevertheless, when Billy Boyle finally parks the car, Epstein puts on a vest before shrugging back into his overcoat. He's thinking he must look ridiculous, an overgrown kid in a snowsuit. But then he sees Billy Boyle and knows the truth. They look like what they are, a couple of nervous cops.

Epstein and his partner draw their weapons before Epstein rings the bell for apartment 4F. Paulie Margarine's responds immediately. 'Yeah?'

'It's Mr Wolf,' Epstein says. 'And Rudolph the red-nosed reindeer.'

Inside, they take the stairs, climbing the three flights. Paulie is waiting in a doorway at the end of a short corridor when they emerge. Automatically, Epstein's eyes rake the gangster, from his naked scalp to his tasseled loafers. Epstein's attempting to read Paulie's body language, but he's too slow. Before he can render a judgment, Billy Boyle closes the distance between Paulie and himself.

'Cover the door,' he tells Epstein. Then he spins Paulie around, pushes him against the wall and frisks him.

'Take it easy,' Paulie says. 'I got bad knees.'

Billy Boyle's response is prompt. He lays the barrel of his Colt against the back of Paulie Margarine's head and slides his free arm around Paulie's neck. 'You're goin' in first.'

Epstein finds himself waiting for Billy Boyle to make some kind of verbal threat. *If there's anybody inside, I'll . . .* But Paulie seems to get the idea. He allows himself to be pushed through the door, pushed from room to room, closet to closet, until Billy Boyle is satisfied. Epstein merely follows behind.

They complete their search in Jane Carter's tiny second bedroom, where her brother sleeps. The apartment is empty, thanks be to God. Epstein's breathes a well-earned sigh of relief, just as Paulie spins around and pushes Billy's gun away.

'Enough is enough.' The gangster stares at Billy Boyle for a moment, then smiles. 'After all, it ain't like you're a couple of honest cops. It ain't like you're only doin' ya job.'

Epstein takes charge at this point, placing himself between Billy Boyle and Paulie. He holsters his weapon, nods for Billy Boyle to follow suit, then waits patiently until Billy complies. It's time to stop doing and start thinking, past time. Still, Epstein takes one precaution. He jams a chair beneath the knob on the front door.

'All right, Paulie, talk to me.'

'I got good news and bad news,' Paulie says. 'The good news is that the problem you dropped into my lap has been handled. Whatever Leonard Carter had on the two of you, he won't be talkin' it up any time soon. Whatta ya think about that?'

'I need the body to be found.'

This is the perfect ending for Solly Epstein. If Carter's body is found, his identity will be determined by a simple fingerprint check, while a comparison of his mitochondrial DNA with the DNA recovered in Macy's will produce a match. Case closed and the bosses happy. Hip, hip, hurray.

'You sure?' Paulie asks. 'Because the package is scheduled to take an ocean voyage in about two hours.'

'Can you stop it?'

'I gotta make a phone call.'

Epstein shakes his head. 'Maybe later. For now, let's talk about the bad news.'

'Forget talkin'. This you gotta see.'

Paulie leads the two cops into the kitchen. He grabs the handle of the freezer door, pauses for effect, then yanks it open. Paulie has arranged Thorpe's hands so that his thumbs appear to be plugging his ears. He's pulled Thorpe's tongue out as well, and forced the man's lips into a wide grin.

Epstein is shocked into virtual immobility. Forget the crime scenes and the mutilated bodies that underlie his professional life. It's as if he's never seen a corpse in his life. For a long moment, he doesn't even recognize Paulie's little touches. He's not surprised, though, when he figures it out. Not by his reaction, or the mocking expression, or by Carter's appearance in the doorway. Carter's holding a shotgun pointed midway between Epstein's and Billy Boyle's faces.

Never give up your gun – you give up your gun, you're gonna die for sure. This is a cop maxim that Billy Boyle has apparently internalized, because his hand disappears beneath his coat an instant before Paulie Margarine drives a well-aimed frying pan into the back of his head.

Billy hits the floor hard. He rolls on to his back and moans. Paulie follows him down, reaching beneath Billy's coat to retrieve his Colt. A moment later, Paulie's holding Epstein's Glock as well. Epstein doesn't protest. But he doesn't wilt, either. He feels as if he's finally come to the end of a long journey, every step of which was laid out in advance. It's not the ending he hoped for, but he's still relieved.

'How'd you do it?' he asks Carter.

'Do what?'

'Get into the apartment.'

'I rappelled from the roof to a bedroom window. One I knew would go up without making a noise. I knew that because I oiled the track a few hours ago.'

Carter motions Epstein to join him in the doorway. Together, they watch Paulie Margarine secure an unresisting Billy Boyle with several rolls of duct tape. 'This is killing my knees,' Paulie tells Carter at one point. But he doesn't stop, encircling Billy Boyle from his ankles to his shoulders before finally hauling himself up. Then he drives his foot into Billy Boyle's gut.

'Put a gun to my head, you cocksucker? Like I'm a fuckin' punk on the street?'

Carter steps between Billy Boyle and Paulie, as Epstein did a few minutes before. He hands the shotgun to Paulie and says, 'Business before pleasure.'

Paulie nods, then turns to Epstein. 'In the living room, on the couch. I want you to sit on your hands in the middle of the couch and I want you to cross your feet at the ankles.'

Epstein tells himself, even as he moves forward, that this might be his last, best chance. He and Paulie are alone in the living room and Paulie has the shotgun pointed at the body armor covering his chest. Will that body armor stop a shotgun blast? Epstein's only sure it'll do a better job than his head. He's sure, too, that once he sinks into the cushions on the couch, he'll be out of options. The only problem is that Paulie's too experienced to be taken by surprise. He's hanging back a good six feet and the shotgun's an autoloader, which means a second shot will follow the first by maybe half a second.

'Something you might wanna consider,' Paulie says. 'If it was up to me, you'd already be dead.'

Epstein sinks into the couch, his hands sliding between the cushions. Helpless, he watches Carter drag Billy into the living room, then return to the kitchen. A moment later, Carter returns. He's carrying a black trash bag which he places beneath Billy Boyle's head. The better, obviously, to handle the upcoming mess.

Twenty-Six

Carter retrieves the shotgun before sitting on a chair opposite Epstein. He seems perfectly relaxed. When Billy Boyle attempts to spit on him, but comes up dry, he smiles a genuinely amused smile. Paulie stands off to the side, holding Billy's automatic in his right hand. He stares at Billy Boyle with an intensity Epstein instinctively associates with lust. Meanwhile, Billy can't keep his mouth shut.

'Fuck you,' he shouts. 'Fuck you, fuck you, fuck you . . .'

'Stop being an asshole,' Carter finally says. 'When Thorpe made his pitch, you could have said no. But not only did you take the money, you tried to kill me twice, even though I warned you after the first attempt. Now you have to accept the consequences.'

But Sergeant Boyle's in no mood to philosophize. He strains against his bonds, hopelessly as it turns out. The duct tape shows no sign of giving way, or even loosening. It's more like Billy Boyle's a spoiled brat throwing a temper tantrum in his playpen. All that anger, it has to go somewhere. Billy Boyle doesn't stop fighting until his face is scarlet and his hair matted with sweat. To Epstein, he looks as if he's about to pass out.

'Lieutenant Epstein?'

'Huh?' Epstein looks up to find Carter smiling.

'Last time we met, I told you not to return. Do you remember that conversation?'

'Yeah,' Epstein admits, 'I recall.'

'So, what happened?'

'Look . . .'

'Didn't you tell me your wife was pregnant?'

'Yeah, I did.'

'Was that true?'

'Yes . . .'

'Do you know how hard it is for a kid to grow up without a father? Do you have any idea?' Carter pauses, but Epstein doesn't reply, though he himself was raised without a father. After a moment, Carter adds, 'You have to say something. This is your chance.'

'Say something?' Epstein's tempted to laugh out loud. 'All right, how about this. If you let me go, you'll never hear from me again. Cross my heart and hope to die. Catholic fucking honor.'

Paulie Marginella grins, revealing yellow teeth and a coated tongue. 'Ya believe this jerk's got an attitude?' he asks Carter. 'I mean, here's a cop, swore an oath to uphold the laws of the land, then peddled confidential information to a murderer. And when that didn't work out, he sent another murderer, yours truly, to kill the first murderer. Now he comes across with an attitude.' Paulie nudges Billy Boyle with the toe of his shoe. 'See, that's what I hate about cops. The arrogance. They got one set of rules for themselves and another set for everybody else. They think their shit don't stink, even when they got diarrhea.'

But Carter's not listening to his partner. 'I believe you,' he tells Epstein. 'If I let you go, I think you'll get the message this time.'

Epstein's heart takes a little jump. Does this mean he can afford to hope? Suddenly, Epstein realizes that it's about much more than his wife and son-to-be, about more than home, hearth and career. Every cell is his body is screaming the same message. Solly Epstein wants to live.

But then Carter adds, 'Of course, that's what I thought the first time.'

'What do want me to do, beg?'

'It ain't a question of what we want right now,' Paulie chimes in, 'because right now I could make you suck my dick. The issue is what you're gonna do later on. If there is a later on, which I keep tellin' my associate is unnecessary, not to mention stupid.'

'How can I prove what I'll do in the future? It's impossible.'

'Not true, Lieutenant,' Carter says. 'You're not out of options yet.'

Epstein looks from Carter to Paulie. They're playing him, the two of them. Good cop, bad cop. The effect is disconcerting, but unless Carter's a sadist – and Epstein doesn't think he is – there has to be a point. Epstein decides to plead his case.

'What we were thinking, originally, was that you'd eventually be identified,' he explains. 'That's not true any more. The DNA evidence we recovered in Macy's was only good for mitochondrial DNA, and the images on the surveillance tape at the Orchid Hotel were too faint to enhance. Look in the pocket of my coat. I have a sketch created by one of our artists. It doesn't look anything like you.'

'Throw me the coat.'

Though Carter doesn't bother to raise the shotgun from his lap, Epstein moves slowly and carefully. He tosses the coat to Carter, who removes the sketch, unfolds it and laughs out loud. Paulie takes a quick look, then he laughs, too. 'You look scarier than me,' he tells his partner.

Carter ignores the remark. 'Last time we met, you told me that you were trying to kill me because I was about to be arrested. So, what's your excuse this time? If I was free and clear, why did you send Paulie after me?'

There's a two-word answer to this question: Billy Boyle. Epstein wants to say the words, as he wants to survive, but he finds himself struck dumb. It's one thing to sell the badge, another to rat on your partner.

'Nothing to say?' Carter asks. 'Well, don't worry your head, because I already know the answer. You, Lieutenant Epstein, you're like the dog who jumped into the swimming pool. Damn, but that water looked good. Only now you don't know how to get out. You're tired and you're drowning and you can't find the steps. Not without help.'

Carter pauses for a moment, then gestures to Billy Boyle. 'Tape his mouth, Paulie.'

Billy Boyle resists when Paulie tries to gag him. He twists

his face away and jerks back and forth like a trapped snake, cursing Paulie with every breath. Although Paulie smacks him in the ear with the Browning, he continues to fight, and Paulie has to hit him again before he settles down. Billy Boyle's not unconscious, though. He's laying on the rug, staring up at his mentor, his rabbi, his hook. He's looking right into Solly Epstein's eyes when Paulie runs a strip of tape over his mouth and around his head.

'Do you see my problem?' Carter asks.

'Yeah.'

'Say it, Lieutenant Epstein. Say it out loud.'

Epstein tries to stop himself, but the words slip out anyway. 'Billy Boyle.'

'Is that what you call him? Billy Boyle?'

'Mostly.'

'Well, it's perfectly clear that if I let Billy Boyle go, he'll be planning his revenge before he starts his car. That's because he's not like you. He's not the dog who jumped in the pool. Billy Boyle's been swimming in that pool for ever. The water is all he knows.'

Epstein finally tears his eyes away from Billy's. He glances at Paulie, who's staring back at him as if he was a rat in a maze. Epstein agrees with Carter's bit about the dog in the pool, especially with how it applies to himself. Not for a minute does he deny that he's about to sink. No, no, no. Epstein's difficulty is with the price of his rescue.

'So Billy Boyle has to die,' Carter persists. 'Do we agree on that? Billy Boyle has to die and Lieutenant Epstein has to kill him.'

Epstein's head jerks up as Carter gets to his feet and crosses the room. He watches Carter open the center drawer of a small desk and remove a semi-automatic handgun, a compact .22 with a silencer screwed into the barrel. As Epstein knows well, the .22 is an assassin's weapon. Fired into a man's skull, its rounds break into small fragments that ricochet through the brain without creating a messy exit wound. Early in his career, while still on patrol, Epstein had been first to arrive at the scene of a homicide. The

entrance wound in the victim's scalp was so small that he
initially suspected a heart attack.

'At another time,' Carter says, 'I'd just disappear. Trust
me, I'm good at disappearing. But the way things are, I
have to stick around. I have to stick around and I can't be
watching my back every minute.'

Carter walks up behind Epstein. He lays the .22 on the
couch and steps away, lifting the muzzle of his shotgun.
Without being asked, Paulie takes up a position six feet to
Carter's left.

'You'll have to jack a round into the chamber,' Carter
says.

Epstein picks up the .22. He yanks the slide back, then
hesitates long enough to check the clip. Only when he's
sure the magazine is full does he release the slide. The
weapon is now ready to fire. And Epstein's ready, too, though
he hasn't yet decided on a target. Paulie Margarine is
standing to Epstein's left. He's holding Billy Boyle's 9mm
semi with the barrel pointed slightly down. Epstein is certain
he can turn and fire at least two shots into the gangster's
torso before Carter pulls the shotgun's trigger. No matter
how well-trained, there's always a gap between the deci-
sion to act and the action taken. The gap isn't very large.
With practice, it can be brought down to a quarter of a
second. Nevertheless, that gap is the major reason why the
man who gets off the first punch generally wins the fight.

But not even at the furthest extremes of his imagination
can Epstein envision taking out both men. If he turns on
Paulie, he's as much as committing suicide. Still, there's a
consolation prize in play. Should Carter pulls the trigger
on that shotgun, a dozen fingers will be dialing 911 before
Epstein hits the carpet. It's Christmas, everyone's home and
the building's solid middle-class. This is not a neighborhood where the roar of a shotgun is likely to go unreported.

Epstein finally turns to Billy Boyle, whose bulging eyes
appear almost demented. Is he terrified? Or still enraged?
Epstein's not sure. But Billy's inner state is irrelevant,
because the only certainty is that whatever choice Epstein
makes, Billy Boyle will die.

Suddenly, Carter steps forward to lay the shotgun's barrel against the back of Epstein's head. 'Can't have you shooting Paulie, can I? Now that I've grown fond of him.'

'You read minds?' Epstein asks.

'No, I calculate probabilities and act on them.'

And there it is, out in the open. Epstein did calculate the probabilities after his first meeting with Carter. And not just once, either. If he'd acted on them, he'd be home with Sofia.

'What you gotta think about is this,' Paulie Margarine adds. 'You got a wife and a kid on the way. What happens to them if your body is never found, if you vanish without a fuckin' trace? Your old lady might not even collect your pension, fa Christ's sake.'

Epstein ignores the gangster. Paulie's definitely not running the show. 'You were wrong about the pool, the one with the dog,' he tells Carter.

'How so?'

Epstein feels something within his soul begin to revolve, a cauldron, heavy and leaded. He feels the cauldron slowly empty, feels himself slowly fill, and he wonders what happened to his heart. That's because it now seems as remote, theoretical and finally irrelevant as the black holes that dot the universe.

'There are no steps in that pool,' Epstein explains as he pushes the barrel of the .22 into Billy Boyle's ear. 'There are no steps and no rescue. In that pool, you swim or you drown.'

Twenty-Seven

Everything old is new again. The words reverberate through Epstein's mind when he finally steps on to the sidewalk. I'm an alien from another galaxy, he tells himself. I've never breathed this air before, never heard the steady hum of a passing airplane, or marked the sharp line of a rooftop against the night sky, or faced into an unrelenting winter wind. *Everything old is new again.*

But not for Billy Boyle. In a few hours, Billy Boyle's remains (along with Montgomery Thorpe's head and hands) will begin a slow voyage aboard a garbage scow. This voyage won't end, according to Paulie Margarine, until Billy's remains are a hundred miles from land, until he rests on the ocean floor beneath two miles of water.

The night has become strikingly cold, the air even more dry and clear. Small clouds scud across the heavens, from north to south. At another time, before he was dropped into this new world, Epstein might have compared them to an armada on the move. But not tonight. Tonight he's thinking the clouds are lemmings in search of a cliff.

Epstein chuckles. Imagine their disappointment, he tells himself, when they discover the Earth is round.

An SUV passes, a Jeep, and Epstein stares at the driver as if at a mirage. The man is elderly and alone. Though he drives with both hands on the wheel, the Jeep weaves slightly, to the left and to the right. Too much Christmas cheer. Though Epstein doesn't know why, he waits until the car turns at the end of the block before setting out for a bus stop on Woodhaven Boulevard. Epstein's on foot because Billy Boyle's Chrysler 300 is also destined for a sea voyage. Within a few days, the Chrysler will be in the hold of a ship sailing under the Panamanian flag. Three days after that, in Guatemala, the car will be unloaded and its identifying numbers removed prior to sale. Again, according to Paulie Margarine, whose eye for the bottom line Solly Epstein finds unnerving.

Epstein catches a bit of luck on Woodhaven Boulevard when a gypsy cab happens by. The cab is piloted by a black man whose thickened English betrays his African origins. He asks no questions when Epstein directs him to a water-front promenade that runs along the harbor near the Brooklyn side of the Verrazano Bridge.

The drive takes only a half-hour and Epstein's content to stare out the window. Queens and Brooklyn are entirely prosaic on their southern ends. Squat apartment buildings, six and eight stories high, one- and two-family homes, store-front businesses with their shutters drawn, the occasional open gas station closer to the airport. Epstein finds the monotony comforting. He knows he's in need of grounding, and this is very familiar ground to Epstein, who spent most of his childhood in nearby Sheepshead Bay.

Epstein slides a fifty dollar bill out of his pocket when the driver finally halts the cab inside a small parking lot. He tears the bill in half and gives one of the halves to the driver.

'I'll be gone about thirty minutes,' he explains.

'You sure die your death of cold,' the driver tells him.

Epstein smiles the first smile of his new life. Africans hate the cold even more than Latinos. You see it in their faces on the first cool days of autumn, a profound misery that won't be dispelled until the following June.

'Don't worry,' Epstein tells the man. 'I was an Eskimo in a past life.'

The driver shakes his head. He hands Epstein a wool cap. 'Put this on your head, mon. Don't play the fool.'

Outside, Epstein pulls the hat down over his head and ears, then slides his hands into his pockets. He's standing underneath the Verrazano Bridge, staring out between the massive towers at the bridge's deck, a narrowing ribbon of black running almost to a point at the far end. Epstein's home is less than a mile away and he's been here many times, occasionally with Sofia, but more often alone. This is where he comes when he needs to think.

Shoulders hunched, Epstein trudges ahead, absorbing the smell and the taste of the sea with every breath. He listens to the waves slap against the sea wall and to the predatory howl of a police siren that somehow penetrates the steady hiss of the wind. In the distance, a chopper crosses the bay, headed for Newark Airport, looking to Epstein like a firefly on a summer's night.

The sounds and smells ease the turmoil. Epstein's not seeking absolution. His problem is much simpler. The urge to unburden himself is threatening to overwhelm him. He has to deal with it before he does something really stupid, like confess to Sofia.

Epstein walks a quarter of a mile, to a bend in the promenade where the entire harbor opens up. His eyes seek the familiar landmarks: Ellis Island and the Statue of Liberty, the skeletal cranes on the docks of Bayonne, sleepy Staten Island across the bay. To his left, the cables of the bridge trail from slender towers that rise to form arches at the top. Epstein has always considered the Verrazano to be the most graceful of the city's many bridges. From the beginning, he was drawn to the span's isolation. The East River bridges that link Manhattan to Brooklyn, Queens and the Bronx succeed each other like the chains of necklace. The Verrazano guards them all.

Turning his head away from the wind, Epstein takes a step, then stops abruptly as a thought flips into his consciousness, agile as a gymnast. If the bosses decide against releasing the Macy's Killer sketch, Solly Epstein will just have to leak it to a reporter he knows. The important thing here is to deflect the investigation.

Epstein pounces on the thought. Yes, Virginia, he tells himself, there is a future. Merry Christmas to all, and to all a goodnight.

Other considerations follow. Epstein finds them consoling, if not particularly pleasant. The Macy's Killer will not be apprehended and Billy Boyle will vanish under suspicious circumstances. Solly Epstein won't be around when Billy's disappearance comes to light because tomorrow morning, citing his wife's difficult pregnancy, he intends to take a leave of absence. A prevailing belief that Epstein knows more than he's telling will inevitably develop, Solly Epstein and Billy Boyle having been all but joined at the hip.

Epstein chuckles. Suspect in a probable homicide? Not good for the old career. But there is one consolation. The next time he meets Paulie Margarine, Paulie's gonna think, If this cop whacked his best buddy, he surely won't hesitate to kill me. And Paulie Margarine will be right, too. Maybe Leonard Carter's too much for Solly Epstein. Not so Paulie.

Ahead of him, Epstein watches a tugboat punch its way through the whitecaps. He's thinking it's about time to go. His face and hands are numb and the cold is eating into his chest. But then the cell phone in his pocket begins to vibrate and he feels a momentary surge of panic. He reaches for the phone, nonetheless, and manages to fumble it open. The call is from Sofia, from his own home just a few blocks away.

'Hey, baby,' Epstein says.

'Have you got a cold? You sound hoarse?'

'No, I'm OK. I'll be home in a half-hour.'

'That's where you're wrong, *mi Corazon*. Meet me at the hospital. Our son is on his way.'

Epstein fills his lungs with air cold enough to hurt. Again, the words tear through his mind: *everything old is new again.*